TREX

Also by Christyne Morrell

Kingdom of Secrets

TREX

CHRISTYNE MORRELL

Delacorte Press

Text copyright © 2022 by Christyne Morrell
Jacket art copyright © 2022 by Karl James Mountford

All rights reserved. Published in the United States by Delacorte Press, an imprint of Random House Children's Books, a division of Penguin Random House LLC, New York.

Delacorte Press is a registered trademark and the colophon is a trademark of Penguin Random House LLC.

rhcbooks.com

Educators and librarians, for a variety of teaching tools, visit us at RHTeachersLibrarians.com

Library of Congress Cataloging-in-Publication Data
Names: Morrell, Christyne, author.
Title: Trex / Christyne Morrell.
Description: First edition. | New York : Delacorte Press, [2022] | Audience: Ages 8–12. | Summary: "A mystery following Trex, a boy with an experimental implant, Mellie, a reclusive girl training to be a spy, and their adventures together as they're pitted against middle school bullies, their own parents, and an evil, brain-hacking corporation"— Provided by publisher.
Identifiers: LCCN 2021018380 (print) | LCCN 2021018381 (ebook) | ISBN 978-0-593-43324-9 (hardcover) | ISBN 978-0-593-43325-6 (library binding) | ISBN 978-0-593-43326-3 (ebook)
Subjects: CYAC: Mystery and detective stories. | Brain—Fiction. | Implants, Artificial—Fiction. | Middle schools—Fiction. | Schools—Fiction.
Classification: LCC PZ7.1.M67265 Tr 2022 (print) | LCC PZ7.1.M67265 (ebook) | DDC [Fic]—dc23

The text of this book is set in 12-point Life LT.
Interior design by Ken Crossland

Printed in the United States of America
10 9 8 7 6 5 4 3 2 1
First Edition

For Edmund,

who taught me everything

I know about superheroes

CHAPTER 1

Trex

I don't expect the fireworks, but I have to admit, they're pretty cool. All bright blue and crackly. Under different circumstances, I'd be impressed with myself for having made them. But under these circumstances—the ones I've been stuck with for as long as I can remember—it's anything but impressive. It's downright dumb. If Mom were here, she'd yank me out of this garden in a flash for making such a spectacle of myself. In fact, she'd probably yank me out of this town altogether and squish my dream of ever being a normal kid. Normal kids don't shoot fireworks out of their fingertips.

But I've never been very good at "normal."

Lucky for me, Mom's not here. Nobody is. I whip my head around to make sure the coast is clear, then sigh in relief. Only Barnaby saw what just happened, and he's not telling because . . . well, he's a dog. He stares at me with his head cocked in confusion. He wasn't expecting fireworks, either.

"Don't give me that look," I tell him. "That was *your* fault."

Barnaby had lunged at something—a squirrel probably—and since I'm on the other end of his leash, he pulled me right along with him. I had no choice but to reach out for balance, and the only thing nearby was a statue—a bronze figure of a girl standing guard in the middle of the garden with one arm raised to the sky. I braced myself for the sting that happens every time I touch metal, like the snap of a rubber band against my skin. It's annoying, but I'm used to it by now. It happens twenty times a day. But I'm definitely *not* used to fireworks.

"That was . . . weird," I mutter, checking for burns and flexing my fingers. They look the same as always—slightly red and calloused. You'd never know they just produced lightning. Or whatever that was.

If dogs can roll their eyes, that's what Barnaby does next. Maybe he's trying to remind me it was my idea to wander into that garden in the first place. It was my idea to put myself within zapping distance of all that metal just for a better view of Hopewell. Even the statue itself—looking down at me with a stern expression on her face—seems to think it was a bad move. Maybe she's right.

But how could I resist? From that garden on the hill,

the town of Hopewell is spread out below me like a picnic blanket. Like the opening credits of a TV show: houses lined up in neat rows, a leafy-green park, a cobblestoned town square. It's perfect. I scan the landscape for a specific building—one that's brick and boxy and not quite as beautiful as all that other stuff. Except to me. Because that boring brick box is Hopewell Middle School, and starting tomorrow, it will be *my* school. I roll the words around in my mouth like a Jolly Rancher. "My school."

On TV, kids are always trying to avoid the place, but as far as I'm concerned, school is like Disney World and the go-kart track and the ice cream shop all rolled into one. It's a land of brightly painted lockers, where I'll roam the halls with my new friends, getting into mischief (the harmless kind, of course) while teachers wag their fingers at us. I'll form lifelong friendships and learn important lessons and have "the best years of my life." At least that's how it is on my shows.

But most of all, I'll be ordinary there. Not the homeschooled kid who spends all day with his mother. Or the kid who nearly died when he was little. Or the kid who technically *did* die, if only for a few seconds. Or—worst of all—the kid who does that weird *thing* with his hands. I'll just be Trex. Plain and ordinary. It's going to be awesome.

If I can pull it off.

If I can make it a whole day without causing a light show.

Which is why those fireworks are anything but cool. And if Mom finds out . . .

Barnaby nudges my leg. He's right—it's getting late. Mom will start to worry, and nothing is more hazardous to my normal life than a worried Mom. I guide Barnaby out of the garden with a nod to the statue. The metal shimmers in the setting sun like warm, gooey honey.

When I get home, Mom is sitting at our foldout kitchen table, surrounded by towers of unpacked boxes. She's eating leftovers from the Plate of the Union Café, where she just finished a shift. She's still wearing her ridiculous uniform—a crisp white shirt, blue suspenders, and a sparkly red bow tie. In every new town—and there have been *lots* of new towns—Mom finds work at the local diner. The quality of the food varies, but the outfits are always cringe-worthy and the puns are even worse: New Fork City. Mad Platter Café. Chew Chew Train. You get the idea.

"You're back," she says, like she's surprised. Like she hasn't been tapping her fingernails and waiting for the creak of the front door. "How was the walk?"

"Good," I say. My voice sounds squeaky and unnatural. I wonder if Mom notices.

"Is everything all right, Trex?"

Yep, she notices. If I give her even the tiniest hint that I'm worried about starting school tomorrow, she'll gladly call the whole thing off. And if I mention that I just created lightning out of thin air? Well, I might as well start packing right now. Static electric shocks are one thing. Fizzy blue fireworks are another. *Pull it together,* I tell myself. *It was a fluke. She won't find out. Everything is fine.*

"Everything is fine," I say. I pull on a pair of highlighter-yellow rubber gloves. We have them stashed all over the house, so I don't accidentally shock Mom or Barnaby.

"Are you excited about tomorrow?" she asks. "Nervous?"

"No!" I blurt out. "I mean yes! I mean . . . no *and* yes." I take a deep breath and start over. So much for playing it cool. "Nervous: no. Excited: yes."

"Uhhh, okay." She narrows her eyes. She's on to me. "Everyone gets nervous on the first day of school, Trex. It's perfectly normal."

There's that word again: "normal." What normal kid has to worry about setting fire to his math homework? And don't even get me started on chemistry lab.

Mom smiles, but this time, *I'm* on to *her.* She's waiting for me to crack. Like a criminal on a cop show, sweating under the hot lights in a police interrogation room. "How about a round of Alphabetter?" she asks.

Alphabetter is a game we invented years ago, to cheer each other up. And to calm each other down. The first time we played, we were in a cheap hotel in Albuquerque with a broken TV and no internet. Or was it Phoenix? Either way, it was someplace hot. To make ourselves feel better, we took turns naming our favorite things in alphabetical order. It's hard to be upset when you're making a list of things you love. But if I agree to play now, she'll know I need it. She'll know something's wrong.

"No thanks," I say. "I'm good."

Instead, the three of us curl up on the couch and watch TV in silence. Well, not exactly silence. I'm wrapped in a rubber blanket, and it makes an annoying squelchy sound every time I move. I'm also resting my head where I can hear both of their heartbeats. Mom's is slow and steady like a rocking chair. Barnaby's thumps around like a tennis ball loose in a closet. Both are comforting in their own way.

One of my favorite shows is on—a hidden camera show where kids play pranks on unsuspecting grown-ups—but I'm too distracted to pay attention. I recite tomorrow's strategy in my head one more time: *Release excess charge as often as possible. Keep my keys within reach at all times. Never remove my lucky baseball cap. Avoid handshakes and high fives. . . .*

I have to get it right tomorrow. I can't get caught off guard again.

I add a new rule to the list: *Absolutely, positively no more fireworks.*

CHAPTER 2

Mellie

When people are doing something they don't want to get caught doing, they look left and they look right, but they never look up. That's why I've got such an impressive collection of other people's secrets. Like the time I saw Mr. Patterson pick his nose and wipe it on his fancy gray pants. Or when I spied Isaac Burns kissing Arabelle Jones behind the rosebushes. I've never seen a murder or anything like that, but I'll bet even Sherlock Holmes had some pretty dull cases when he was twelve, like *The Mystery of the Missing House Keys* or something. Even the best of us have to work our way up.

Lucky for me, I live at the peak of Hopewell Hill, with the best view in town. My house is a crumbling old dinosaur, but it's three stories high, and my room is all the way at the top. It used to be the attic before I claimed it. I wanted to be the tallest thing in Hopewell, to see everything there was to see, so I pushed aside the old boxes, swept up the cobwebs, and made it my own. It's still a little musty, but it has room to spare, and it doesn't look so gloomy now that Mother painted it yellow. (The particular shade gives me a headache, but she swears it's the most cheerful of colors.)

I know how I must seem from down there—the girl in the shadows peering through her curtains at the world below, like a phantom from a creepy Victorian novel. I have half a mind to wear a flowing white dress and howl at the moon just to play the part. But someday, when I solve a really big case, people will nod and say, "Now it all makes sense. Good thing she honed those detective skills when she had the chance." Until then, they'll smirk and whisper about poor, reclusive Mellie the Mouse.

The real reason I'm stuck up here, though, is because I'm sick. Or sick-*ly,* you might say, since the doctors can't pin down what's wrong with me, let alone find a cure for it. That's why I spend hour after hour staring down at the shiny bronze scalp of the statue in the center of the garden, the Unnamed Girl. She has a severe sort of face, with high cheekbones and thin lips that refuse to smile. Everyone else in town thinks she looks mean, but I quite like her.

Besides, you can hardly blame her for wearing a grumpy expression—she's always getting stepped on. Climbing all the way up the raised arm of Unnamed Girl is the ultimate dare in Hopewell, even though one boy allegedly fell off and broke his leg. You'd think the threat of fractured limbs would keep kids from trying to scamper up the statue, but it actually has the opposite effect. Middle schoolers are like that, though—completely immune to reason.

Speaking of unreasonable, I was watching from my window the day Harrison Palmer tried to make the climb. With his minions cheering him on, he scaled the statue all the way to her waist, as the hot, slippery metal tried to send him sliding back down. Even from where I stood, I could see the panic in his eyes as he glanced down at the solid ground seven feet below him. Conveniently for him, the Sweeney twins' mother called them home at just that moment and Ridley Duncan discovered something on her phone more interesting than Harrison's antics. As soon as he realized he no longer had an audience, Harrison whooped and triumphantly scooted down the statue's skirt. At school the next day, he boasted to everyone that he'd climbed all the way to the top, stared into the empty eyes of the Unnamed Girl, and given her frozen hand a high five. Ridley stood beside him, confirming his harrowing story. Even the Sweeney twins—who were nowhere near the statue at the time—nodded along like lemmings.

Meanwhile, I knew the truth, but I didn't say a word.

Because I don't just collect secrets. I keep them, too.

But the boy walking beneath my window doesn't strike me as the type with anything to hide. He must be the new kid, the one who moved into the blue house down the hill with the white picket fence. He looks about my age, with white skin and sandy hair that sticks out the sides of his baseball cap. He's wearing a T-shirt, basketball shorts, and sneakers. In other words, he's entirely unremarkable. Just like his dog—a beast so mutt-like I can only classify him as a "dog."

They wander into the garden and stare out at Hopewell, mesmerized. Then the unremarkable dog goes after a squirrel, and the boy reaches out to the statue for balance. Just as his skin is about to come into contact with the Unnamed Girl, a bright blue zigzag passes between his hand and her metal boot. A streak of light, like a spark. Only bigger. Much bigger.

A firework.

I gape out the window, not even bothering to shrink behind the curtains. Am I really seeing what I think I'm seeing?

I *must* be. My eyes never play tricks on me. They're my most reliable body part.

The boy wiggles his fingers, and the spark dances along the edge of the statue's boot, like a jagged snake charmed by his fingertips. When he lifts his hand, the light grows to almost a foot in length, sputtering and hissing and changing shape. The boy doesn't flinch or yelp in pain, and I can't tell if he's terrified or pleased with himself.

I reach for my notebook. But what do I write? What am I watching?

The boy curls his fingers into his palm, and just as quickly as the light appeared, it dissolves. The new kid seems rattled but not as much as he should be. Why isn't he freaking out? With a parting nod to the Unnamed Girl, he and his mutt march out of the garden.

I stare at the statue for thirty minutes after that, waiting for her to do something. To burst into flame or come to life or . . . something. But she doesn't. So I pace the length of my room, thinking. There has to be some logical explanation for what I just saw, some secret this boy is hiding. Maybe he's not so unremarkable after all. The new kid is a mystery waiting to be solved—and solving mysteries is what I do best.

I pace and puzzle over him for so long I almost forget that tomorrow is the worst day of the year: the first day of school.

When I finally fall asleep, I dream of electric-blue lightning in a sky without rain.

CHAPTER 3

Trex

Just as my hand is about to hit the doorknob, I spin around. Barnaby needs one last tussle before I head to school. Or maybe I do. But instead of a slobbery Barnaby, I come face to face with a stone-faced Mom. She's cradling a mug of coffee and giving me a lifted-eyebrow, are-you-sure-you-want-to-go-through-with-this? look. Even though I'm sweaty and jittery, like a soldier about to march into battle, I *do* want to go through with it. So I give Barnaby a quick scratch behind the ears with a plastic back scratcher, adjust my lucky baseball cap, and charge out the front door.

Straight into a group of middle schoolers.

Four kids my age are passing in front of my house, all decked out in their backpacks and crisp first-day-of-school clothes. They're heading down the hill, toward Hopewell Middle School, but they stop in their tracks when I step outside. It's like one of those cowboy movies, where a stranger wanders into the local saloon and all the conversation stops and the music screeches to a halt. And then the biggest, baddest outlaw in town walks over with his fingers in his belt loops and his boot spurs jangling, to check out the new guy.

In this case, the outlaw is a pale kid with tangled blond hair and splotchy red cheeks who breaks from the group and stomps over. The new guy is me.

"I'm Harrison," says the blond kid. "Who're you?" His expression is a cross between a smile and a sneer, like this is a test and he's waiting for me to give the wrong answer.

"Trex," I say. "I just moved here."

"Trex?" he repeats, his grin widening. I've done exactly what he wanted. "What kind of name is Trex?"

"Uh . . . ," I mumble. I can't argue with him. What kind of name *is* Trex? Why didn't my parents name me Jack or Steven or something? Why'd they have to be so annoyingly creative?

Harrison raises his pale, insistent eyebrows. The others watch with smiles creeping onto their faces.

"I—I'm named after a dinosaur," I say. I sound like a six-year-old. I *feel* like a six-year-old. Maybe it's not too late to duck back inside and forget the whole going-to-school thing.

"A 'Trex' isn't a dinosaur," Harrison points out. He looks at the other kids and smirks.

"It stands for *T. rex*," I say. *"Tyrannosaurus rex."*

Harrison's grin fades. "I know what a *T. rex* is. Duh."

"That's an awesome name!" says a Black boy wearing track pants and a matching jacket, and the other kids chime in to agree with him. I silently forgive my parents for their annoying creativity. Only Harrison seems unimpressed. The kids invite me to walk to school with them, and I try not to sound too excited when I accept. As we start down the hill, they pelt me with questions:

"Why are you named after a dinosaur?"

"Is it because of your large head?"

"Or your tiny arms?"

"Or because you've got an insatiable appetite for blood?"

"Um . . . no," I say, suddenly self-conscious about several different parts of my body. "My dad was a paleontologist. He studied dinosaur bones."

That receives another round of "cools" and "awesomes," which makes Harrison's face pucker like he just did that viral lemon-eating challenge and regrets it. Nobody seems to notice that I talk about my dad in the past tense.

"I'm Ridley," says a white girl with a mane of shiny blond hair, wearing a pleated plaid skirt and patent leather Mary Janes. She pauses and holds her hand out to me for a handshake. I freeze. Five minutes into my attempt to be normal and I'm already busted. Luckily, the same boy who complimented my name darts between us.

"I'm Ben," he says to me. As his tracksuit suggests, he seems to be in perpetual motion—leaping onto the curb, kicking rocks—and I wonder how he'll survive in a classroom all day.

"Excuse you!" yells Ridley, pushing him out of the way. "*I* was talking to Trex!" While they're playfully shoving each other, a Black girl with the same brown eyes as Ben slips in and introduces herself.

"I'm Danica, Ben's twin sister," she says with a nervous giggle. Unlike her brother, she moves slowly, like she's trying not to crease the fabric of her dress or mess up the perfect ponytails on either side of her head.

"Nice to meet you," I say.

Behind us, I hear a creak and the long, low whine of hinges. A door opening. I glance back at the house on top of the hill, a three-story monstrosity, all gray and spiky, that belongs in a horror movie. I can already tell it's haunted. There's a sudden blur of movement, and a girl slips out the front door. She perfectly matches the house, with almost translucent skin, scowling eyes, and limp black hair falling over half her face. She moves like a cat burglar making an escape.

"Who's that?" I ask.

"Who?" says Ben, peering over his shoulder. "Mellie the Mouse?"

"She never walks to school with us," says Danica. "She hardly even *goes* to school."

"I'm surprised you even noticed her," says Ridley.

But Harrison spins around with a mischievous gleam in his eye. "Check it out!" he booms. "A Mouse sighting!" He charges back up the hill toward the girl.

Mellie stiffens. She pulls her elbows in close and presses her chin into her chest. She's small to begin with and is doing her best to make herself even smaller. She reminds me of the roly-polies that hide under Mom's flowerpots. As soon as the sunlight hits them, they go from busy little bugs to solid balls of armor.

"May we walk you to school?" asks Harrison, swooping in next to her. His voice drips with sugary sweetness. It makes my skin crawl.

"She's very delicate," says Ben, rushing over to join in. "I think she needs a bodyguard."

"I'm fine," mumbles Mellie, keeping her head down. Her voice is barely a whisper, as creaky as her door hinges. Harrison and Ben are on either side of her now, boxing her in.

"Really?" asks Harrison. "Why do you miss school all the time? What's wrong with you?"

"My mom says she's making it up," Ridley whispers to me, loud enough for everyone to hear.

"Are you contagious or something?" asks Ben.

"C'mon, tell us, Mouse," Harrison insists. He's obviously not afraid of catching whatever she has, because he leans in close. "What's wrong with you?"

"Nothing is wrong with me," she says, stumbling away from him.

"Something definitely is," Ridley explains in a know-it-all voice. Which might be her all-the-time voice.

"Tell us, Mouse," hisses Harrison.

"Does she even talk?" Danica giggles.

"She's so weird," says Ridley, shaking her head as if such weirdness is a terrible shame. I feel sorry for the squirming girl. I've been called weird more times than I can count. I wonder if I should help her, maybe create a distraction or something. But then she looks up from under that curtain of hair and points.

At me.

"I saw him last night in the garden," she says, her voice suddenly clear. "And something strange happened."

CHAPTER 4

Mellie

I try to warn the new kid. When he spots me slinking out of the house, I glare at him from under a protective layer of hair. "Keep walking," say my eyes. "Nothing to see here." But apparently our eyes don't speak the same language. So obviously I blame him for everything that happens next.

Harrison runs toward me with a cruel smile on his face. In the background, the others watch like they're at a play and the curtain just rose. They nudge each other and whisper excitedly. Only the new kid has no reaction at all.

Harrison has always enjoyed teasing me, ever since we were in elementary school, but he's never gone out of his way to do it. I'm just not that important. *Why now?* I wonder.

Then it dawns on me: Harrison is showing off, marking his territory. He's threatened by the new kid. And just by stepping out the door, I've become part of his act. The unwitting victim.

"Why do you miss school all the time?" Harrison sneers. "What's wrong with you?"

"Are you contagious or something?" asks Ben, shoving his face in front of mine. I bet his cheeks would turn as red as Harrison's if I told his friends about the spiral-bound sketchbook in his backpack. About how he skips track practice to "do his homework" when he's really drawing the Unnamed Girl in the garden.

"Does she even talk?" chirps prim-and-proper Danica. Her secret? She still plays with dolls. Which isn't so bad, as far as secrets go, but she's named them Harry, Ben, and Ridley, and she's constantly devising clever ways to maim them. Her favorite method involves the magnifying glass from her science kit, which burns perfect black holes into their fabric.

"She's so weird," adds Ridley. Ridley's got the most scandalous secrets of all. She lives in the fanciest house on Hopewell Hill, which got egged last year by some "hooligans," according to Ridley's father. Actually, it was just one hooligan, who was mad at her parents for grounding her and taking away her new bike. They never did catch the culprit.

I know all these secrets and more. With just a few words, I could put any of these kids in their place. But I don't. I go after the new kid instead.

"I saw him last night in the garden," I say. "And something strange happened. A bolt of electricity shot from his fingers to the statue. Or maybe from the statue to him. But it didn't seem to hurt him. It was almost like . . . like he made it happen."

I didn't set out to expose him—especially before I've made sense of him—but the words come tumbling out. Maybe because his secret is the only one that baffles me, and I want him to offer up a simple explanation. Or maybe he's just the easiest target.

Or maybe I turn on him because he's standing there with his hands in his pockets, just like the others. And for some reason, I thought he'd be different.

"That's crazy," he says, his jaw clenching. "She's making that up."

"I told you she was weird," says Ridley.

"It's cute that you're trying to impress us," says Harrison, "but Trex is new here. It's not cool to make up stories about him, Mouse."

"She really is nuts," says Ben. "It's worse than I thought."

"I know what I saw," I say, a faint nausea curdling in my stomach.

"I get that you want attention," says Trex, "but it's a little desperate, isn't it, Mouse?" My eyes snap to him, and he ducks my glare with flushed cheeks—whether from anger or shame, I can't tell. The others sneer at me and congratulate him. He's one of them now.

"You're lying!" I say. My voice trembles. In fact, all of me is trembling. An ache tightens in my stomach like a fist. *Not now,* I beg my belly. *Anytime but now.*

"It's pretty obvious who the liar is," says Trex.

"Wait until you hear what she did in second grade," says Ridley. "She—"

I scream.

Ridley falls silent. They all do.

I keep wailing as the fist clamps down and pain rips through my midsection. The last thing I see before I double over is Trex's face, his eyes round with fear.

"Let's get out of here," says Ben.

"C'mon," says Harrison. "She's not worth it."

"Don't worry," Ridley assures Trex. "She does this. A lot."

I groan as the knots inside me twist tighter and tighter.

"Run!" someone shouts—I can't tell who. The kids break into sprints, and all I hear after that is the pounding of shoes on the pavement and my own blood rushing through my ears. When the thumping fades, I'm alone, bent in half in the middle of the street, my long hair sweeping the dirty asphalt.

CHAPTER 5

Brick

Hopewell hasn't had rain in weeks. Everywhere I go, people have the drought on their lips. *When do you think it'll rain? My hydrangeas are wilting away. Blah blah blah* . . . The air is brittle and scratchy, like dry leaves ready to ignite, and I'm afraid a strong wind will scatter me like sand. But I carry on because there is work to be done. Important work.

I stand behind something called a Little Free Library. It's a box where people leave their old books so other people can take them, read them, and pass them on. That's the sort of town this is—one where they give stuff away for free, right on the street corner. Adorable, right?

That's one way to describe it. If you ask me, people who share books probably share too much. This is probably the sort of place where everybody knows everybody else's business, and you can't make it ten feet down the sidewalk without having to stop and chat about . . . I don't know . . . grass and the weather, I guess. That kind of chumminess was never really my thing. And it could be a problem.

I pretend to be fascinated by other people's discarded books. Mysteries, romance novels, the odd Western—all of them shabby and torn, read and reread. Who has time for such nonsense?

From under the brim of my baseball cap, I watch them.

I won't pretend I'm any good at this spy stuff. I wear a long coat even though it's a humid mid-August morning. I wear sunglasses even though the sun is barely risen. I must look ridiculous, but I was never trained for this sort of thing. Then again, I wasn't trained for much of what life has thrown at me. Yet somehow I manage.

But when all those kids surround her, and when his face contorts like that, a thick Russian tragedy tumbles out of my hands and lands in the dirt with a thud. I didn't see that coming. When the shrieking begins and they all run away, I forget myself. I turn to watch, straight on.

I almost blow my cover.

CHAPTER 6

Mellie

With each stab of pain, I picture the teacher's red pen slashing up, down, and across. An accusing red *A* in the attendance book. *Absent.* Soon I'll have a row of them, just like last year. One for each time I crumple up and limp home. The front door swings open before I make it up the porch steps, as if Mother expects me back already.

"Oh no," she says, guiding me in. She's wearing her fluffy pink bathrobe, with her hair twirled up inside a pink towel and piled on top of her head. She looks like a cone of strawberry frozen yogurt. "Oh no, oh no, oh no."

"I know, I know, I know," I reply. I stumble to the recliner in the living room and curl up in the soft dent in the leather. Like everything else in our house, that dip in the cushion is there on purpose, molded precisely to Father's backside. There's nothing haphazard about the Chandler home. Father likes everything in its proper place, like columns of numbers in one of his ledgers. If he were in the living room right now, he'd say that kids belong in school, not curled up in leather butt prints. Then he'd frown at the pools of shower water Mother dripped onto the hardwood floor.

"Mother?" I whimper.

"Oh no," she says again. She tightens the belt of her robe until I think she'll squeeze herself in two. She doesn't rush upstairs for the chalky pink medicine or the chalky blue medicine or the runny kind that smells of peppermint. She just stands there, fiddling. Dripping.

"The medicine . . . ?"

"But, darling . . ."

"You need to call the school . . ."

"Remember what your father said . . ."

"And get my homework assignments . . ."

"That if this happens again . . ."

"I need some ginger ale, room temperature . . ."

"We'd have to see the doctor . . ."

"Do we have soup?"

"The real doctor."

"Mother!" I manage to sit up, just so I can glare at her.

"I'm making an appointment," she says.

"But, Mo—" The cramping cuts my sentence short. I collapse back into the chair.

Mother presses her hand to her heart. Or the spot where one used to be. "I'm sorry," she says, blinking fast. "It's time."

She rushes off in a pink blur to call the doctor, and I hobble up the stairs to my room. Being sick is no reason to neglect my work. Especially since I have a new case to investigate. *The Case of the New Kid.* No . . . *The Mysterious Matter of Lightning Boy.* That has a nice ring to it. Every case needs a catchy title. Especially since they'll all be in my memoir one day.

I crack my bedroom window open for the morning news. The Mom Squad is gathered outside, speaking in hushed, urgent tones. They cluster at the top of the hill every day to gossip and keep an eye on their young kids—in that order. They're an excellent source of leads, even if their information does require a lot of fact-checking.

"Did you see him?" asks Mom #1. "The creepy guy standing by the Little Free Library?"

"I did!" squeals Mom #2. "At first I didn't think anything of it. A coat in August is a little strange, but sometimes I throw a coat over my pajamas when I take Doodle for a walk, so who am I to judge? But the way he was watching those kids . . ."

"A trench coat, sunglasses, and a baseball cap?" adds a third Mom. "It's just too much! Like something out of a novel! Can you imagine, someone like that prowling around Hopewell Hill?"

"I, for one, am going to keep an extra tight rein on Spencer from now on," says Mom #1. "Spencer! Get away from that lawn mower!"

"He was staring at the middle schoolers. That's for sure," says Mom #3.

"Speaking of middle schoolers," says Mom #2, "did you hear the Chandler girl screaming? It was enough to wake the whole neighborhood!"

I slam the window shut. I have all the details I need: trench coat, sunglasses, baseball cap. I jot it down in my notebook. Now I just need a title. *The Case of the Hopewell Hill . . . Creeper?*

Stalker?

Prowler?

Yes, *Prowler*. Sherlock would approve.

And then it dawns on me: if the Mom Squad is correct, then this criminal—this Prowler—was spying on *me* this morning. A new type of commotion stirs inside me, but it's not the usual stomachache this time. It's more like bubbles fizzing up in a soda. I think it might be . . . excitement. This Prowler doesn't know what he's up against. *I'm* the one who does the spying on Hopewell Hill.

And I'm the one who's going to catch him.

First a kid with superpowers moves into the neighborhood, and now this?

Professionally speaking, sixth grade is turning out to be very interesting indeed.

CHAPTER 7

Trex

School hasn't even started yet, and already I'm toast, thanks to Mellie Chandler. Even as I call her a liar, I feel my skin tingling and my charge building. I clutch the keys in my pocket so tightly they cut into the fleshy part of my palm. But it won't be enough. Soon everyone will get a live demonstration of Mellie's so-called "lie." And my whole attempt at being normal will be over before it begins.

Then Ben shouts, "Run!" and I do. I sprint all the way down Hopewell Hill. As the blood rushes through my veins, the sizzling fades away. But the image of Mellie sure doesn't. She's in my head, folded over, howling like a wounded animal.

It's not my fault she's sick, I remind myself. She was sick before I got here. And it's not my fault the other kids don't believe her stories. She's the one who goes around spying on perfectly innocent people. Everything that happened this morning, Mellie brought on herself.

When I finally spot Hopewell Middle School up ahead, the vision of Mellie Chandler disappears. I careen to a stop on the wide green lawn, where kids are milling around in groups, chatting and roughhousing and showing off. It's exactly like I pictured. I turn to my new friends, and only then do I realize that they're no longer with me. Oops.

Harrison chugs up to me first, huffing and puffing. His cheeks are even redder than before, like an overripe tomato about to burst. He doesn't look happy. Ben and Ridley show up next and promptly collapse on the grass. Danica, barely jogging, is way behind us.

"Wow, the new kid can run!" pants Ridley.

"Yeah, you were flying," says Ben.

"It was mostly downhill," grumbles Harrison.

"Do you run track?" asks Ridley.

"No."

"Do you play any sports?" asks Ben.

"No."

"What about clubs?" asks Ridley.

I shake my head.

"So what *do* you do?" asks Danica, arriving fresh-as-a-daisy to the conversation.

"Well . . . I . . . uh, watch TV. And play video games. Have you guys ever heard of *Legends of Oren*?"

"The one where you pretend to be a warlock?" Harrison smirks. "That's so nerdy. You play that?"

"No," I say quickly. "That was just an example. Of a game I *don't* play."

It's my all-time favorite video game, but no way am I going to admit that now.

"So TV and video games are all you do for fun?" says Ridley. Her know-it-all voice is replaced with an I'm-not-impressed voice.

"Actually, I'm going out for track this year," I blurt out. "So . . . yeah . . . track. Track is my thing."

Oops again. Mom isn't going to like this one bit.

"Awesome," says Ben, brushing the grass off his clothes. "There's a sign-up session during lunch today. I guess I'll see you there." He lifts his palm for a high five. A completely ordinary gesture that sends me hurtling into a panic. My keys are in my pocket, but they might as well be on another planet. If I don't touch something metal, I'll zap him for sure. And the more I worry about zapping him, the worse the zap will be. "Don't leave me hanging," jokes Ben.

Just when my lack of response is starting to get really weird, it comes to me. I curl my fingers into a fist and hold up a row of bony knuckles. Ben is confused at first, but then he grins. Our knuckles collide. No zap. No jolt. Nothing.

"We mostly did fist bumps at my old school," I say.

"Fascinating," says Harrison, rolling his eyes. "Now let's get this over with."

As if Harrison has given them their cue, all the kids on the lawn begin to shuffle toward the building. I barrel toward the front door, pretty pleased with myself for the fist bump idea. Now I just have to avoid touching anyone else for the next seven hours. And for the whole school year. And for the rest of my life . . .

"Hey, Dino-boy!" calls Harrison. Without realizing it, I've bounded ahead of the others again. I'm almost to the school's double doors when Harrison waves me back. Have I broken an unspoken rule by entering the building before him? He's flashing me that smug look again. "You know you can't wear that in school, right?"

"Huh?" is my brilliant reply.

He points to my head. To my lucky baseball cap.

"Yeah, duh," I say, removing the hat and slipping it into my backpack. "Everyone knows that."

I had no idea. Suddenly the door in front of me is like a portal into another world, a world with an entirely different set of rules. And no matter how many TV shows I've watched in preparation for this moment, I still don't know them.

CHAPTER 8

Mellie

I pummel the shiny floor with my sneakers, hoping to make a scuff in Dr. Colson's perfect marble tiles. With its fancy sofa and useless throw pillows, the lobby looks more like our living room than a doctor's office, which is why Mom flinches whenever I touch anything. She lays her hand softly on my knee, to stop me from kicking.

It's not that I mind doctors as a general matter. I'm definitely used to them by now. But Father has decided that I'm suddenly old enough for a "real" doctor, which is why we're in Dr. Colson's Pottery Barn showroom instead of Dr. Sweeney's scruffy waiting room with the train set in the corner and *Highlights* in the magazine rack. When I politely informed Father that pediatricians like Dr. Sweeney go to medical school, too, he rolled his eyes and said that Dr. Sweeney hadn't solved the problem, so it was time we try something else. Then he disappeared into his office, and that was the end of the discussion.

"Mrs. Chandler?" calls the receptionist. She wears a suit and too much makeup, and her blond hair is knotted into an elaborate twist. I miss the staff at Dr. Sweeney's office, with their messy buns and scrubs with puppies on them. At least they dressed like medical professionals there. What bothers me most about Dr. Colson's office is that it's a fraud. No matter how fancy the furniture, they're still going to poke you with needles and make you pee in a cup. Who do they think they're kidding? As soon as Mom gets up to talk to the front desk lady, I start kicking again.

When we're finally admitted to the inner sanctum, Dr. Colson rises to greet us. He's a tall white man with dark hair and bushy eyebrows to match. His grin is so wide it crinkles his eyes in the corners and stretches his cheeks like Silly Putty. "Melissa!" he cries, as if we're best friends, even though we've never met before. I scowl at his outfit: a plaid shirt with rolled-up sleeves and a vest on top. He looks like he should be going for a hike, not offering medical advice. He ushers us in, and Mother and I sink into his upholstered chairs. There's a sign on the wall behind his desk that says: *It's not what you look at that matters. It's what you see. —Henry David Thoreau.* That doesn't even make sense.

The suit lady offers us a "beverage" but frowns when I ask for room-temperature ginger ale. She brings me a bottled water instead. When she's gone, Dr. Colson leans back in his swivel chair, teepees his fingers, and studies me with a serious expression. "So, Melissa, I hear you're having some gastrointestinal issues."

I nod. So he read the intake form. Big deal.

"Tell me about it," he says.

He makes it sound so simple. But it isn't.

It's a stomachache, but it's *more* than a stomach-ache, too.

It happens without warning, like I'm sitting on one of those carnival dunk tanks above a tub of cold water, waiting for the ground to fall out from under me. No matter how much I brace myself, the plunge always takes me by surprise.

And the fall is dizzying. And the slap of the water stings like sharp knives.

And then I'm submerged in a Plexiglas tank, gulping for breath but getting a lungful of liquid instead.

And beyond the partition, there are people—talking and laughing and eating cotton candy—but when I reach out to them, I bump up against a clear wall. Everyone is close and far away at the same time. And I can't get to them, no matter how hard I try.

It's a stomachache, but it's more than that. Because when I'm having one, I'm . . . somewhere else. I'm alone.

"They feel like . . . stomachaches," I say, setting aside

my rather brilliant extended metaphor. Dr. Silly Putty wouldn't understand.

"They're awful!" adds Mother. "We've tried everything to address them, but nothing seems to work."

"Hm," says Dr. Colson, lifting his chin and staring down the slope of his nose at me. "How often do they occur?"

I shrug. "Once or twice a week."

"Is there anything in particular that triggers them?"

"Not really," I say, squirming in my seat.

Dr. Colson nods again. His face has now settled into a look of intense concern. He leans forward, with his elbows on his desk, and asks Mother, "Do you mind if Melissa and I speak privately for a few minutes?"

My eyes dart to her. "Of course not," she says, but she seems flustered as she gathers her things. I resist the urge to grab her by the wrist and make her stay. I know I'm too old to have my mother hold my hand at the doctor's office, but Dr. Sweeney never made Mother leave the room. She gives me an encouraging nod and shuts the door behind her.

Dr. Colson leans back in his chair and exhales. Somehow he's even more casual now that Mother is gone. "How's school, Melissa?"

"It's Mellie," I say flatly.

"Mellie," he says. "Tell me about school. Are you making friends?"

"Um . . ." Why does this guy need my whole life story

just to diagnose a stomachache? I bet my parents are paying him by the hour. "School's fine. Yeah, I'm making friends."

"Who do you sit with in the cafeteria? When I was a kid, your spot in the cafeteria meant everything." He smiles at me like we're having a moment. We are *not* having a moment.

"Well, today's the first day, and I'm here so . . ."

"What about last year?"

"I ate lunch in the library," I say. "I like to read."

"Did you sit with anyone in the library?"

"Of course. My friend Myrtle."

"Wonderful," he says. "I know you've heard this before, but it's very important that you attend school on a regular basis. Not only for educational purposes, but it's critical to your *blah blah blah . . .*"

Okay, he doesn't really say *blah blah blah,* but he keeps talking.

And talking.

I don't understand how all this blabbering is going to help. He doesn't even prick my finger or take an X-ray or press down on my belly to see where it hurts. Occasionally he'll toss out random questions, like "What do you eat for breakfast?" or "If you could have any superpower, what would it be?" I don't see the point, but I spit out answers, just to get it over with. And even though he agrees that invisibility is the best superpower and he's read all the Greenglass House books, he's obviously a quack.

Luckily, I've perfected the skill of multitasking, essential to any detective who finds herself suffering through pointless conversations with adults when there's work to be done. So while Dr. Colson is busy yapping, I put my mental energy to better use. Namely, solving my cases. A good detective is never off the clock. In my head, I run through the evidence for *The Case of the Hopewell Hill Prowler* and *The Mysterious Matter of Lightning Boy.* I plot my next moves. I ponder—

"Does that sound like a good plan?" asks Dr. Colson.

Uh-oh. I look over at Dr. Colson's giant clock and see that nearly an hour has passed. Dr. Colson is staring at me, waiting for me to respond.

"Uh . . . will it make the stomachaches go away?" I ask.

"That's the idea," says Dr. Colson. "Though it may take some time."

"Okay," I say.

"Excellent!" He beams at me. "We've covered a lot of ground today, and I know it can be confusing at first. I'm going to send you home with some reading material. Take a look at it when you're ready. I'm always here to talk, even between appointments."

He slides a glossy brochure across the desk. On it, there's a photo of a group of kids, walking arm in arm with joy on their faces. The sky behind them is a brilliant blue, the grass an emerald green. They remind me of the Hopewell Hill kids on their way to school. The girl screaming into the pavement must've been cropped out. I stuff the brochure into my pocket and mumble, "Thanks."

When Dr. Colson walks me back into the lobby, Mother hops up quickly, like a puppy who's been waiting for her owner. "Well?"

"She was a champ," said Dr. Colson, smiling at me like we're in a secret club. "I'd like to see her again in a couple of weeks. And if you're up for it, it helps if the entire family attends some of these sessions with Mellie, especially early on."

"Really?" asks Mother, furrowing her brow like he just suggested we bring the queen of England to my next appointment. "Is that necessary? My husband and I both have really busy schedules these days."

"I see," says Dr. Colson. "Perhaps that's something we can consider for the future, then."

"Yes, of course," says Mother, brightening. "And what about the stomachaches? Is there something you recommend to help with those? A prescription?"

"I'd like to see Mellie a few more times before we discuss medication," he says, clapping a hand on my shoulder. "To get a better sense of what's at the root of the problem."

Mother gives him a tight smile, the one she uses when she's trying to be polite but doesn't mean it. "It's just that . . . she misses so much school. My husband and I were hoping . . . well, we want to get her feeling better as soon as possible so she doesn't fall behind."

Dr. Colson nods, relaxing into a Silly Putty grin again. I wonder if I reach out and poke his cheek if my fingertip would make a dent. "I understand," he says. He slides a prescription pad from the pocket of his khakis and removes a pen from somewhere in his vest. Maybe he wears hiking gear for all the handy little compartments. He scribbles something onto the paper, but I can't make out what it says. "This should help with your symptoms," he says to me, even as he hands the prescription over to Mother. "We'll start small, and if this doesn't work, we can always make adjustments. Sometimes it requires a little trial and error to find the right fit."

"Thank you, Dr. Colson," says Mother, with a smile so broad it now rivals the doctor's. I don't understand what all the smiling is about. It's just a doctor's appointment.

"Call me Dr. C," he says as he walks us toward the door. I groan. How can I possibly take this guy seriously?

We head back through the spotless lobby, Mother beaming at me and clutching my new prescription like it's a winning lottery ticket. I note with pride two thick black scuff marks on the polished floor.

CHAPTER 9

Trex

Mom holds a steaming mug of tea and leans across the kitchen table. Barnaby rests his head on my knee, his ears poking up like the old-fashioned TV antennae we have to use at hotels that don't have cable. Both of them are completely engrossed in the tale of my first day of school. I tell them about navigating the maze of hallways and the confusing slip of paper that is my schedule. I tell them about my teachers—the funny ones, the trying-to-be-funny ones, the strict ones, the boring ones. I tell them about the cafeteria, and how I sat with the Hopewell Hill kids smack in the middle of the room—like we were the sun and everyone else was orbiting around us.

"Lunch was the best!" I say. "I traded my string cheese for a cherry Fruit Roll-Up. Where have cherry Fruit Roll-Ups been all my life?"

"You poor deprived child," says Mom with an amused

smile. "I'm glad school and its snacks lived up to your expectations."

"I'm glad it lived up to the good ones," I say. "I didn't want to mention it before, but I was kind of nervous about school."

"No kidding," says Mom. "I'm pretty sure you fed Barnaby a bowl of Cheerios this morning."

"That explains why my breakfast tasted funny," I say with an exaggerated grimace. "So you noticed I was nervous and you didn't freak out?"

"I freaked out a little," she says, "but one of us had to keep it together. So . . . can I freak out a little bit now?"

"Sure," I say. "You've earned it."

"Did you feel all right today?" She places one of her hands on top of mine. Through my thin rubber glove, I feel the heat of her skin, still warm from the tea mug. "Did you pace yourself? A real school day is so long. If you need me to, I could stop in during lunch—"

"Mom!"

"Okay, okay, I won't show up at school. Just being . . . a mom. Sorry."

"I didn't have any problems today. It's going to be fine. I promise."

She nods. She seems calm. Maybe even convinced I can pull this off. I guess it's as good a time as any to break the news.

As casually as I can manage, I say, "I think I'm going to join the track team."

"What?" Her eyes grow wide, and her hands flutter to her sparkly red bow tie, as if it's suddenly choking her. There goes her calm.

"It's not a contact sport, Mom. It'll be fine."

"It's a bad idea, Trex. What about something less vigorous? Have you considered the chess club?"

"I talked to the track coach during sign-ups, and he's really excited about me joining the team. Ben told him how I sped down Hopewell Hill on the way to school. He even said I could show up a few minutes late to practice so I could walk Barnaby in the afternoons." Barnaby gives a little whimper, as if he doesn't want any part of that lie. The truth is, I'll need time to recharge before practice since I'm not allowed to wear my lucky baseball cap at school. But Barnaby has no reason to complain—at least he'll get a walk out of it.

"You promised you'd keep a low profile," says Mom. "We both know how you can run when you're at your best. Somebody will notice—"

"I'll let the other kids win a race or two," I say with a grin.

Mom doesn't answer. She simply dunks the tea bag up and down in the hot water. Barnaby moves his head from my leg to hers. He always knows who needs it most.

"It was eight years ago," I say softly. "They're not going to find us. They're probably not even looking anymore."

"You don't know these people," she says. "They're ruthless. They won't stop until they get what they want."

She means me. *I'm* what they want.

And *they* is The Company.

The Company operated on me after our car accident. The Company replaced my damaged brain with an awesome, experimental one. The Company saved my life. But, apparently, they didn't do it out of the goodness of their hearts. When the surgeries were over, they insisted on keeping me in their lab for observation and to run a few tests on my fancy new brain. But Mom wouldn't hear of it. So The Company brought in their lawyers, who informed her that, in the chaos after the accident, she'd signed an agreement that said The Company owned all the equipment in my head. They basically owned *me.* And, according to Mom, they intended to collect.

So we ran. And we kept running. And we keep my brain a secret in case The Company ever comes looking for us. But no matter where we go, Mom sees them—men with hats pulled low over their faces, lying in wait in alleys and dark corners, ready to pounce. I'm all for real life being like a movie, but evil scientists hiring thugs to chase us all over the country so they can experiment on my brain? That's too far-fetched, even for me.

I place my hand on top of Mom's. It isn't as comforting with a squelchy rubber glove on, but I think it helps anyway. "Apple pie," I say. I can tell she needs a round of Alphabetter right now. Maybe we both do.

"Um . . . bow ties," she says, pulling off her patriotic neckwear with one sharp yank. "But *not* this one."

"Candy canes. Two points."

"Dogs!" says Mom, giving Barnaby a good scratch behind the ears.

It's working. She's almost smiling again. So what if I leave out a few minor details of my epic first day? Like the fact that my electrical charge—an annoying side effect of my high-tech brain—is changing. Getting stronger. Or that Mellie the Mouse saw me electrocute a statue and almost ratted me out to the most popular kids in school. Or about Mellie howling in pain in the middle of the street, because of me.

"Easter eggs," I say.

"Friends," says Mom.

"Friends," I repeat under my breath, the word like a light bulb flickering to life over my head. Now there's an idea. I can't do anything about my charge, but maybe there's a simple solution to my other problem—my Mellie the Mouse problem. It won't be pleasant, but it just might work.

I have to become *friends* with Mellie the Mouse.

CHAPTER 10

Brick

This part of the job—following a couple of kids back and forth from school—should be easy. But who am I kidding? Nothing about this job is easy. Just when I think I've got the hang of it—putting on this ridiculous getup, hiding in the shrubbery, avoiding the nosy moms—the kid goes and joins the track team, and I have to re-arrange my whole schedule. This is why I never wanted children of my own. So inconsiderate.

Even so, I adjust. By the end of the first week, I know their movements. I even know their moods. In the morning, the boy walks to school with the other kids, joking and laughing. If I didn't know any better, I'd think he was just like them. A normal kid. The girl, meanwhile, peers out the window and waits for them to leave before she dares to set foot outside.

In the afternoon, though, it's a different story. He's

the one who hangs back. He avoids those other kids, separates himself from them. He walks with heavy feet and stooped shoulders, like the day has drained the life out of him. And the girl? She stays on his tail, on the opposite side of the street, never taking her eyes off him. She slows when he slows, pauses when he pauses. Sometimes she jots down notes in a spiral-bound book. He turns around often, like he knows she's there, but she always ducks behind a tree or a trash can. Watching them makes me chuckle. It's almost comical—the fact that I'm not the only spy on the block.

Almost.

I may not have trained to be a spy, but I know a thing or two about lying. The Company taught me how to lie like a pro, until lies slipped out of my mouth as naturally as my own breath. At times, I think about pulling these kids aside and warning them about a life like this. About how difficult it is to live in a world built on fiction. How, after a while, you forget what the truth looks like. Sometimes I wish someone had done that for me.

But I don't tell them anything. I keep quiet and do my job.

CHAPTER 11

Mellie

"Breakfast!" Mother calls up the stairs. "And don't forget to take your pill!"

I shake one of the little pink pills onto my palm and size it up like it just challenged me to a duel. It's shiny and unassuming. Cute, even, like a button or those licorice-flavored candies Father used to get at the baseball stadium. But this is no treat. This is a pill you have to swallow whole, the kind that lodges in the back of your throat. The kind that is supposed to make me feel better. That is supposed to make me *normal*.

I type the unpronounceable name of the pink pill into my computer and pull up a list of side effects longer than *The Mysterious Benedict Society* (which happens to be the longest book I've ever read). As I scroll, a few key words catch my eye: "drowsiness, difficulty concentrating." Suddenly the stomachache/dunk tank doesn't seem so bad. I vaguely recall that Dr. Colson mentioned something about this when he was rambling on and on. Did he say that the side effects are mild and usually temporary? Either way, it's a risk I can't take. A detective has to be on top of her game at all times. I can power through a few more stomachaches if it means rooting out the Prowler and uncovering the truth about Trex Wilson. I drop the pink pill back into the bottle.

I slide my earbuds into my ears so Mother won't distract me with conversation, but I don't turn on any music. I need to think. I grab a bagel, plop down at the kitchen table, and flip open my notebook. If there's one good thing about my parents forcing me to go to school every day, it's that I can gather more evidence about Trex. I reread my notes on *The Mysterious Matter of Lightning Boy:*

1. He can shoot lightning from his fingers.
2. He can run really fast without getting tired (according to Ben).
3. He wears a ratty old baseball cap, which he claims is "lucky."
4. He gives everyone fist bumps.
5. He walks home alone after school.
6. He's different at the end of the day. Tired? Sad?

"Mellie? Honey?" Mother raises her voice over my nonexistent music, which startles me out of my thoughts. I pop out an earbud. "It's time to go."

"I'm going to be home late today," I say, slinging my backpack over my shoulder.

"Oh," she says, brightening. "What for?" She's obviously hoping I've joined a club or—god forbid—a sport. I decide to have a little fun.

"I'm going to track practice," I say. Mother's eyeballs nearly pop out of her head.

"Track? Wow . . . I didn't know you were interested in running! That's fantastic, honey! Do you need new sneakers? We could go to the store this weekend."

"It's purely for research purposes," I add, slamming my notebook shut.

"Oh," she says, deflating. "What sort of research?"

But I've already reinserted my silent earbud.

I don't hear another word.

CHAPTER 12

Trex

I jog up to the track, only to be glared at by a bunch of sweaty red faces. "Nice of you to join us, Dino-boy," says the reddest face of all. Harrison lobs a wad of spit onto the track, and it bubbles there. *Of course* this is Harrison's sport. Maybe I should've gone with the chess club after all.

"Sorry," I say. "I got here as fast as I could. It's just . . . the dog . . ." I imagine how these kids would react if I told them the truth—that if I didn't go home and charge my artificial brain, I wouldn't make it halfway around the track without powering down like a robot.

"Save it," says Harrison. "The rest of us have been warming up for the last fifteen minutes, so you need to catch up. Why don't you start with . . . hmm . . ." He grins. "The 1,600."

"O-okay," I stammer. "Should I tell Coach Russell I'm here?"

"Not necessary," says Harrison, puffing up his chest to match his cheeks. "I'm team captain. I pretty much run practice."

"Oh." I drop my things on the bench, stalling as I look for Coach Russell.

"Well? Are you waiting for an invitation?" asks Harrison.

I shake my head, jog to the track, and plant my sneakers on the nearest white line. I can feel the other kids staring at me as I crouch into position. But as soon as I burst from the starting line, the world around me becomes a blur. Including all those judging faces. The wind makes my eyes water and tangles my hair. My legs pound against the springy surface of the track. I charge around the oval once. Twice. Three times. It's like I'm running downhill again. I'm flying. And best of all, my fingers aren't tingling. No metallic taste in the back of my throat, no electronic buzz in my ears. I feel almost normal. I don't even notice all the kids—and Coach Russell—trying to flag me down every time I pass.

I finally chug to a stop right where I started. Even before I turn around, I feel a change in the boys behind me. They're still gaping at me, but the skepticism has been wiped off their faces. A few of them whistle and raise their eyebrows. Some of them even smile. But not Harrison. He sucks on his lips, which makes him look like a splotchy, toothless old man.

"Son!" barks Coach Russell, stomping over to me

with his hands on his hips. "What was that?! You're not even warmed up. You could get seriously injured with a stunt like that. Are you trying to pull a muscle?"

"N-no, but Harrison said—" I glance over at Harrison. He gives me a tight, sneering smile.

"You can't be on this team if you can't follow the rules, do you understand?" says Coach Russell.

I nod.

The coach's face slowly softens. "That was impressive, though. You've got real potential. *If* you toe the line."

"Thank you," I say. "I will." Harrison is standing behind Coach Russell, fuming. I avoid eye contact with him.

I stretch and do some warm-ups with the team. When we run sprints, I remember my promise to Mom. I hold back and only beat the others by a few seconds. Still, Coach Russell is beside himself. We run as a herd, but his eyes are on me. Over and over, my times are the best on the team, though I'm barely making an effort.

The fact is I'm not a great runner—smoking the rest of the team is yet another side effect of my implant. The scientists from The Company turned off the pain receptors in my brain so I wouldn't suffer after the accident. Apparently, they never got around to turning them back on. I get the same aches and cramps as everyone else—I just don't feel them. That's why I can run so fast without stopping.

"One more drill before I let you go," announces Coach Russell as a band of sweaty boys huddles around him. "The relay." He's holding four colorful batons—red, yellow, blue, and green. They glint in the sunshine, and my heart clenches.

They're metal.

Coach Russell chooses four team captains and hands out the batons. I've been assigned to the anchor position, so I have time before the baton is passed to me. To panic.

I try to think of an escape plan. I could pretend to be sick. Or fake a call from Mom. But these kids are already annoyed at me for showing up late. How will it look if I leave early, too?

But if I grab a metal baton, I might dazzle them with something other than my speed.

Someone asks Coach Russell a question, and he turns his back, leaving his things lying on an empty bench, just a few feet away from me. His clipboard. His stopwatch. I inch closer.

"What are you doing?" asks Harrison, appearing beside me.

"Nothing," I yelp. "I just wanted to double-check my time on the 800 again."

"Nobody is allowed to look at Coach's clipboard," he snaps, yanking it off the bench.

"Oh . . . right. Sorry."

He walks off in a huff, with the clipboard clasped to his chest. He leaves the stopwatch unattended. This is my chance. I tap it softly with my finger. It only takes a second.

As we jog to the track, my heart is beating at least twice as fast as it should be. If my plan doesn't work, maybe I'll drop dead on the spot. That'd be one way to get out of this relay. The lead runners step up to the starting line and get into position. Coach Russell places the whistle between his lips and raises the stopwatch to eye level.

He frowns. He presses a button, and the frown deepens. "What the . . . ?" he mutters, shaking the stopwatch and mashing buttons. "I just bought this stupid thing."

Coach Russell groans and recalls the lead runners. The first day of practice ends early so he can stop by the sporting goods store. Most of my teammates are relieved as they tromp back to the locker room. But Harrison seems less than pleased. He casts a suspicious scowl in my direction.

As I'm walking away from the track, I realize that Harrison isn't even my biggest problem. Because sitting in the bleachers is a girl in a gray hoodie, so mousy nobody else notices her. And, as usual, she sees everything.

Mellie

"I know you're behind me," says Trex without turning around.

"So what?" I say casually. "This is my way home, too."

"Why have you been following me?"

"Why are you so full of yourself? I'm not following you."

"Then why were you at track practice?" he asks.

He spins around and faces me before I can take cover behind a trash can. My stomach threatens an uprising, but I tamp it down. I clench my teeth and wait for it— the taunts, the name-calling. *Weirdo. Freak.* It's never very original, but it always gets the point across.

"I want to apologize," he says.

"Ummm . . . what?" My gurgling belly relaxes, but not all the way. This might be a trick.

"For what happened on the first day of school. I didn't realize you were . . . you know . . . sick."

"But you lied," I say. "About the lightning."

"Look, I don't know what you think you saw. . . ."

"You know exactly what I *know* I saw."

"People think you're nuts," he says. "You're not help- ing your reputation by making up stories."

"People think you're *not* nuts," I shoot back. "People can be wrong."

"I'm trying to apologize here," says Trex, standing in front of me on the sidewalk now. I glance at him through narrowed eyes. I can't tell what his angle is—yet—but I know he's up to something. A good detective has a sense about these things.

"Apology not accepted," I say. I stomp past him and continue up the hill.

I don't turn around, but I picture him standing behind me, awestruck, wondering what just happened. It makes me smile. But seconds later, I hear his rubber soles squeaking as he jogs to catch up. He's beside me again.

"Now who's following who?" I mumble. I march up to the Little Free Library. The Mom Squad spotted the Prowler there again this morning. It's important to investigate the scene of a crime within hours, if not minutes, after the event, before the evidence is disturbed. But real detectives don't have to spend half the day in middle school.

"So . . . you like books?" he asks as I pull open the creaky door to the tiny library. I ignore him as I work my way through one shabby volume after another—picking each one up, fanning its pages, and putting it back. "That makes sense."

I cut my eyes to him. "What's that supposed to mean?"

"You know. Every school has a bookish girl, a loner type, usually a little sassy."

I roll my eyes. "Not everyone is a stereotype."

"That's exactly what the sassy bookish girl would say."

"Oh yeah? So I guess that makes you the popular jock?" I say, lacing my words with sarcasm.

"I don't know about that. I'm more like . . . the intriguing new kid." I don't look at him, but I can tell he's grinning.

"Being the intriguing new kid eventually gets old, you know."

"Yeah, tell me about it," he mumbles. I stop leafing

through *Diary of a Wimpy Kid* and look over at him. He drops his gaze and kicks at the dirt.

"Where'd you live before this?" I ask.

"Buford, Georgia."

"How long did you live there?"

"Three years."

"Where'd you go to school?"

"Stafford Elementary."

"Who was your best friend there?"

"Gary Perkins." He doesn't miss a beat. It's almost too good. Rehearsed, even. "Why all the questions?"

"Just curious," I say, turning back to the books.

"Which one are you going to pick?" he asks.

"None of them."

"Oh."

He stands there awkwardly with his hands in his pockets, and I let him be awkward. I like the idea of someone other than me being awkward. He clears his throat, and I realize he's not going to leave.

"I'm not looking at these books for fun," I finally say. "I'm working on something. Something important."

"Oh yeah? What is it?"

I hesitate. Is *this* the part where he makes fun of me? Is he being nice to me so he can gather more ammunition for Harrison and the other jerks?

"Well?" He's uncomfortable. Squirming. His secret is right there, ready to be spilled. I just need to lure him in. Maybe even—ugh—become friends with him . . .

"I'm kind of a detective," I blurt out. I regret it almost immediately. Here it comes . . .

"Like . . . a cop?" he asks. He actually seems curious. He's not making fun of me. I think.

"More like Sherlock Holmes," I reply. "You've heard of him, right? He's a character in a book. But don't worry, they make TV shows about him, too."

"Of course I've heard of him. I just didn't realize those kind of detectives were still a thing."

"Crime is still a thing," I say, "so someone has to solve it. Have you heard about the Prowler? The guy creeping around Hopewell Hill in a trench coat, spying on kids?"

"A . . . a prowler?"

"*The* Prowler," I say. "He's been spotted at this location."

"A prowler . . ." His words trail off, and his eyes grow wide. His face drains of color.

He's obviously impressed.

Trex

"Yes," says Mellie. "The Prowler."

Unlike mine, her voice is steady. Bold, even. It's not the same squeak it usually is. And unless I'm seeing things, she's smiling. Actually *smiling.*

"What does the Prowler have to do with those books you're looking at?" I ask. I lean against the solid wood of the Little Free Library, trying to keep myself upright even as the world has gone topsy-turvy.

"I'm not looking *at* books," she says. "I'm looking *for* clues. I'm going to catch him."

She says this with such confidence, I instantly believe her. *Of course* a twelve-year-old amateur detective is going to catch a criminal. Even if that criminal is a hired gun. Even if he's a well-trained, well-paid goon working for a powerful company that will do anything to reclaim its greatest invention, which just happens to reside in the brain of an ordinary-looking sixth grader.

Could Mom have been right about The Company all this time? I suddenly feel unsafe, exposed. I have to do something.

"I want to help," I blurt out.

Mellie turns to me with a steely expression, and I suddenly miss the timid girl peering through her hair. This is an entirely different version of Mellie the Mouse. I'll admit, this one scares me a little. "Why?" she asks.

"It sounds like fun," I say, giving her a too-big, too-desperate grin.

"Fun?" she says, spitting out the word with disgust. "It's not *fun*. It's work. I'm trying to accomplish something here. Solving crimes is serious business."

"I know," I say. "I'll take it seriously."

"No." She slams the door of the Little Free Library so

hard the rusty hinges threaten to crumble. She brushes past me and marches toward her house.

"I watch cop shows!" I call after her. "I've seen every episode of *Perry Mason* with my mom. Some of them twice!" I realize how pathetic I sound, but I can't help it. This is no longer about pretending to be friends with Mellie the Mouse. If there's a prowler on Hopewell Hill, I have to catch him before Mom hears about it. Even if it has nothing to do with The Company, Mom will lose it. Then it's goodbye, middle school and track team and fist bumps and Fruit Roll-Ups. Goodbye, ordinary. If Mom suspects that The Company has found us, our stuff will be crammed in the back of a moving truck by morning. I can't let that happen.

And if it *is* The Company? I don't know what I'll do.

"Mellie Chandler works alone," says Mellie.

"But Sherlock Holmes had a sidekick," I say. "You need a Winston!"

She glares back at me. "You mean a *Watson*?"

"Yes?"

She shakes her head in dismay, then trudges up the steps to her front door.

"I'll tell you a secret!" I cry.

She pauses with her hand on the knob of the front door. "I'm listening."

"I'll tell you something that nobody else in Hopewell knows about me. My deepest, darkest secret." I don't know what I'm going to tell her exactly. Definitely not my real secret. But I'll deal with that pesky detail later.

"Go on."

"I'll tell you *after* we start the investigation."

"Hmph." She twists the doorknob. "How do I know you're not lying?"

"How do I know you're a good detective?" I shoot back. "I don't want to waste a secret like this on a fraud."

Mellie whips around and strides back down the steps, her eyes boring into mine. "Fine," she says. "I'll let you help me on one condition: *I'm* in charge of this operation."

"I wouldn't have it any other way."

"You have to follow my instructions. And you can't say anything to anyone."

"Agreed."

"Good," she says, with a knowing smile creeping onto her lips. "I guess we have a deal then." She extends her hand for a deal-sealing handshake.

"Deal," I say. Before she can change her mind, I take off down the hill. I leave her hand dangling there, unshaken.

CHAPTER 13

Mellie

"Melissa, come here."

No sooner has the front door shut behind me than I'm called into Father's office. His voice is hard, like he's summoning a puppy that just ate his slippers. I gulp and push open the heavy door. I've only set foot in this room a handful of times, usually to fetch Father his reading glasses or a book, darting in and out as though the floor were covered in lava instead of a very expensive Oriental rug. A desk lamp casts a dim yellow light on the imposing wood furniture and thick leather books. The only indication that this room is inhabited by an actual human is a single photo on the bookshelf of Mother, Father, and me, taken when I was about seven. In it, we're in the stands at a baseball game, mugging for the camera. We're wearing matching hats for the local minor league team, the Sparks. We look different. Happy.

In stark contrast to Father's face right now. He sits behind the desk with his hands clasped, every inch an accountant. It's so dark in there, it takes me a moment to notice Mother's slight figure perched at the edge of an armchair.

"Yes?" I whisper. The room seems to demand only whispers.

"I want to speak to you about your health," says Father. "Your mother tells me your condition has been improving since your appointment with Dr. Colson. That you haven't missed a single day of school this year, aside from the first one. Is that true?"

"Yes, sir."

"That's excellent news," he says. "And yet."

Uh-oh. Nothing good ever comes after "And yet."

"This morning your mother made a rather upsetting discovery," he goes on. "While she was tidying your room, she noticed that your pill bottle seemed quite full. So she counted them."

"You counted my pills?" I gasp, turning to Mother. She looks down. Father clears his throat, reclaiming my attention.

"It seems you haven't taken a single one," he says. "Not a single pill since your appointment last week. Do you care to explain?"

"Um . . ." I don't care to explain, actually.

Father sighs wearily. "Melissa, you need to take this situation seriously."

"I—I do," I say. "It's just that, I don't need the pills. I've been feeling really good lately." Which is true, if you don't count the shooting pains I had in English when I found out we had to read our research papers out loud to the entire class. Or the squeeze in my stomach when I thought Jane Pittman was waving at me from across the hallway (it turned out one of her actual friends was standing right behind me). Or the moment of paralysis when I had to cross paths with Harrison and Ben in an otherwise-empty hallway. Besides that, I've been almost symptom-free.

"You're not a doctor," says Father. "You're not in a position to make that determination. We've spent a fortune on your appointments and medication. What's the point of all that if you're going to disregard your diagnosis?"

"B-but the stomachaches haven't been that bad—"

"Enough!" roars Father, and the whole room quakes. I swear I see ripples in the after-work drink on his desk. I seek Mother's eyes, but she's busy studying her impeccable red fingernails. "Everyone in this room knows full well that you don't suffer from 'stomachaches.' You have an illness, Melissa, but it's not a gastrointestinal one. It's time you come to terms with that."

The rug beneath my feet is plush, with intricate patterns that remind me of *Arabian Nights,* another thick volume I read in my room while the other kids played outside my window. Right now, I wish it would fly away and carry me off to a sand-swept place. To anyplace. Away from Sick Mellie and Sick-*ly* Mellie and Mellie the Mouse. And Mellie the Liar.

"Were you even listening to Dr. Colson?" asks Father. "You clearly didn't read the materials he provided. We found this in the trash." He slaps a glossy brochure on the desk. There are those kids again—laughing, their arms linked. "I expect you to take your pills from now on," he says.

"But—"

He raises his eyebrows, daring me to keep going.

I don't. I stare at the rug.

Father sighs, lowers his head, and massages his temples. "We're trying to help you, Melissa. All your mother and I want is for you to go to school and make friends and be . . ."

The sentence trails off, like he's searching for the right word, but I know what comes next. "Normal." Like the kids in the photo. Like seven-year-old me, back when Father still took me to Sparks games. Before I became an embarrassment. A ledger he couldn't balance. A problem he couldn't fix.

"Happy," he adds quickly. "We want you to be happy." Nice save, but I'm not buying it. If he really wanted me to be happy, he'd let me see Dr. Sweeney. And he'd let me stay home when I'm sick. And he'd let me get back to my cases. And he'd leave me alone.

I bite my lip. And my tongue.

"This is for your own good," says Father, his tone softer now. "You can't keep missing school, and you can't stay locked in your room all the time. You're going to take your pills, and that's final. Do you understand?"

"Yes, Father."

"Good," he says. He sighs again and picks up his glass. The ice cubes clink against one another with a delicate *tink-tink* sound.

I take the brochure from the desk, but the tears pooling in my eyes blur the words until I can't read it. The happy kids blur, too, until I can't tell one smiling face from another.

CHAPTER 14

Brick

"Kellerman Vogel's office," chirps Ronnie.

"It's me," I say. "Is he there?"

"Brick!" squeals Ronnie. "How are you?"

"Shhhhhhh!"

"Sorry," she whispers. "Silly me. Where are you, Brick? Somewhere exciting?"

I'm in an alley, sitting on a stoop littered with cigarette butts, beside a garbage dump. It's one of the few places I can have a private conversation around here.

"Ronnie, we talked about this."

"Oh yeah. Top-secret. Hush-hush. I forgot."

Ronnie is a sweet lady, even if she is a few chapters short of a novel. But Ronnie has been with The Company longer than most, and she knows her way around. She's also the boss's secretary, which makes her a very useful resource indeed.

"Is he there?" I ask again.

"No," says Ronnie. "He left yesterday for a grand opening. Very glamorous, I suppose."

"I need you to do me a favor. Can you check the files and send me everything you find on Allan?"

"Allan?" she says, and I hear the tremor in her voice.

"Yes," I say firmly.

"Sure, Brick, whatever you need."

"Hey, Ron, have you ever heard of something called dry lightning?" I ask.

"Hm, can't say that I have," she says. "But it sounds neat."

I'd never heard the term, either, before I came to Hopewell, and now I can't escape it. Along with the drought, it's this town's favorite topic. Dry lightning is a rare and dangerous occurrence that can cause fires and electrical outages, and with the lack of rain, Hopewell is primed for it right now. The effects could be disastrous for my assignment. "Neat" isn't exactly the word I'd use to describe it. "Deadly" is more like it.

"Why the sudden interest in lightning?" asks Ronnie.

"Just . . . a theory I'm working on," I say.

"Did I tell you I got a new puppy?" she asks, changing the subject so quickly it almost gives me whiplash.

"What? No. I have to go. Just get me the files."

I hang up before she can tell me about her schnauzer or the latest exploits of her No-Good Boyfriend. Before she can sigh and make me feel bad about rushing her off the phone. I don't have time for small talk. Not right now.

A situation is developing here. Not only is the weather becoming a concern, but just this afternoon, I saw Trex and the junior detective by the Little Free Library, talking to each other. They looked awfully chummy. Could they be working together? Are they—heaven forbid— *friends*?

This isn't good. That girl is nosy. And smart. She's going to be nothing but trouble.

I'm not sure what's making me more nervous—an extraordinary atmospheric event that could threaten everything I've ever worked for, or a twelve-year-old sleuth named Melissa Chandler.

CHAPTER 15

Mellie

Stafford Elementary is a quaint redbrick school in Buford, Georgia, with an award-winning math team. I click around on their website and don't find anything that disputes Trex's story. But a good detective doesn't stop with an easy answer. She digs deeper.

I dial the school's phone number. When the receptionist answers, I use my best grown-up voice. "Hello, I'm calling from the *Buford Gazette,* local desk. We're running a story on the Mathletes. We understand they took first place at regionals last year and are poised to do it again. My boss asked me to double-check the spelling of the Mathletes' names. Can you help me?"

"Well, of course I can!" says the receptionist. "I'm just tickled you'd write about our math team. That'll show those baseball players that Mathletes are no joke!"

"Yes, ma'am."

"My son Carter is on the math team, so why don't we start with him. The Mathletes always do—ha! It's C-A-R-T-E-R. Last name Jones. J-O-N-E-S."

I tap my fingers on the keyboard to pretend I'm taking it down. "Wonderful. What about Trex Wilson?"

"Excuse me—did you say *Trex*? Is that a nickname?"

"Let me check my notes." I riffle some papers around on my desk. "No, I'm showing here that Trex is the boy's legal name. Trex Wilson."

"Hm, I don't recall anyone by that name on the team."

"He may have been the alternate. And it looks like he relocated at the end of last year. Can you check last year's records?"

"Sure, let me check the system. That name doesn't ring a bell, but I'll confirm."

I hear her typing, then humming as she waits for her computer to respond.

"Just as I thought," she says. "No such student as Trex Wilson enrolled here last year. Not in any grade. And certainly not a Mathlete. But let me go ahead and give you the correct names of the other team members. Okey-dokey?"

As she spells each name, I set the phone down and continue my research. It doesn't take long to discover that Trex's "best friend" Gary Perkins is a short-order cook at a diner in Buford called New Fork City. It seems that Trex really did live in Buford, but he didn't attend Stafford Elementary. And if Trex is lying about that, I can just imagine what else he's hiding.

But one question in particular is still nagging at me. Why would Trex—a kid with so much to hide—agree to work side by side with a detective with such obvious talent? Why would he offer up his deepest, darkest secret? Why was he willing to grovel for the chance to help me?

He's obviously desperate. But *why*?

I open my notebook to *The Mysterious Matter of Lightning Boy.* Then to *The Case of the Hopewell Hill Prowler.* I flip back and forth between the two, waiting for inspiration to strike.

Lightning Boy.

The Prowler.

And then it hits me. I can't believe it didn't occur to me sooner.

What are the odds that the two biggest cases of my career show up at the exact same time? That can't be a coincidence. A good detective doesn't believe in coincidences. There has to be a connection. The Prowler and Trex Wilson are connected. . . .

The Prowler isn't spying on the kids of Hopewell Hill—he's spying on *Trex*!

Which means the Prowler knows Trex's secret. And it must be something serious. Or valuable. Definitely dangerous.

My two cases are *one* case. A case that's going to make a name for Mellie Chandler.

"Will you let me know when the article comes out?" asks the receptionist after she spells the last Mathlete's name. "I'd love to hang it on the fridge."

"Sure," I say. "You've been more helpful than you know."

CHAPTER 16

Trex

When Mellie suggests we go on a stakeout, I jump at the chance. I imagine us posted in the back of a windowless van, chugging cups of strong coffee and blinking groggily at infrared video feeds from inside the bad guys' hideout. When we finally hear them hatching their evil plot, we make our move. They take off. We chase them, leaping fences and dodging barking dogs, in a thrilling pursuit that ends in a dramatic arrest. Or something like that.

In real life, Mellie doesn't have any cool spy equipment, but she does have a full view of the entire neighborhood from her bedroom. We stand at opposite ends, stationed at two large windows. Mellie watches the garden side, with a view of the Unnamed Girl, while I stand guard over the Little Free Library. I spy three cars and two dogwalkers, but that's it. I spend most of the time staring at an empty stretch of street. It's not exactly *Lethal Weapon,* which I managed to watch once before Mom made me turn it off.

"So . . . how long have you been detective . . . ing?" I ask after about fifteen minutes of awkward silence and bored fidgeting.

"A few years," she says.

"What are you always writing in that notebook?"

"The things I notice."

"Like what?"

"You're not going to stop talking, are you?" she asks.

"Nope. Tell me what you notice."

"Ugh, fine," she sighs. "Um . . . a few months ago, I noticed that Mr. Galleki always stopped and tied his shoe in the same spot on the sidewalk every single day."

"So?"

"So . . . sometimes little things like that turn out to be big things."

"Did Mr. Galleki's shoelaces turn out to be a big thing?"

"For Mr. Galleki they were," says Mellie. "He was stopping there on purpose, waiting for Ms. Lewis to come outside with her yappy dog, Walter. And now they're engaged."

"Ms. Lewis and her dog are engaged?"

Mellie groans.

"Just kidding," I say. "That's really cool."

"A good detective pays attention," says Mellie. "It's

not like cases jump out and announce themselves." She shoots me a knowing look. "At least not usually."

"Doesn't it feel wrong, though?" I say, giving that look right back to her. "Spying on people?"

. "Of course not. I'm not peeping into windows or anything. I'm just observing what people do in public, right out in the open. It's perfectly legal."

"Yeah, I know it's legal. But it's still an invasion of privacy," I say, thinking about how a single moment in the garden gave Mellie the power to pretty much ruin my life.

"It's no worse than looking people up on the internet," she says.

I slide my eyes to her, but she's serious about sticking to her post and doesn't turn around. "You stalk people on the internet?"

"Of course. Don't you?"

"No."

"Well, you should. It's the first thing I do when I meet someone new."

"Um . . ."

"Yes," she says. "I googled you. And I didn't find anything. Not a social media account. Not a science fair award. Not a track meet announcement. Not a single solitary thing. And it's not like you have a common name or anything."

"My mom doesn't like me to post things online," I

say. "She'll be glad to know even Mellie Chandler didn't dig up any dirt on me."

"Is your mom one of those off-the-grid types?" asks Mellie. "Please tell me you don't have a bunker in your backyard."

"No, nothing like that. Mom's just . . . cautious." "Paranoid" is more like it, but I don't want to admit that. Especially to Mellie.

"Cautious about what?"

"Everything," I sigh, automatically reaching for my baseball cap and pulling it down low.

"What about your dad?" she asks.

"He died when I was little," I say. "In a car accident. I don't remember much about him."

"It is true he studied dinosaur bones, and that's how you got your weird name?"

"Yep," I say, relieved to talk about the one thing I *do* know about him. Mom gets all choked up when I mention him, so I usually don't.

"Did you know *Tyrannosaurus rex* had hollow bones?" asks Mellie.

"Really? That's random."

"When I searched your name online, it pulled up a bunch of information about *T. rex* instead. I learned that their bones were filled with air sacs to keep them light and buoyant. The *T. rex* needed lightweight bones to support its giant head, which was basically empty."

"I didn't know any of that."

"*T. rex* was the original airhead," she says. "So it's the perfect namesake for you."

I gasp and glance over at her. "Did I hear that correctly? Did Mellie Chandler just crack a joke?"

"Don't get used to it," she says, but her voice is on the verge of actual laughter. And something shifts. It's like all the awkwardness is suddenly sucked out of the room, and I can breathe. Maybe my plan to become friends with Mellie will work after all.

Feeling relaxed, I lean back against her cluttered desk. And I gracefully knock over everything on it. Pens and pencils scatter in different directions, a bobblehead of some minor league baseball player clunks to the floor, and an orange medicine bottle rolls across the uneven hardwood. Mellie shrieks and spins around. She tries to pounce on the medicine bottle, but I reach it first and set it back on her desk.

"Sorry," I say, chasing the rest of the pens and pencils around the room.

"It's okay," she says, swiping the bottle and slipping it into the pocket of her hoodie.

"Is that for your stomachaches?" I ask.

"Yeah," she mumbles, returning to the window on her side of the room.

"What . . . what exactly is wrong with you?"

And just like that, the tension returns to the room.

Even with her back to me, I can tell that Mellie doesn't want to talk about it. The laughter is gone from her voice now. I wish I could take the question back, but it's too late.

"I don't know," she says quickly. "I've been getting stomachaches for years. The doctors aren't sure what causes them."

"Oh," I say. "It must be hard not knowing."

"Yeah," she says softly.

We fall silent again. The awkwardness is back, worse than before. I'm such an idiot. Just when I was finally getting her to like me—or at least to stop hating me—I have to go and talk about medical stuff. Given my own situation, I should know better. And then it dawns on me . . . a foolproof way to cheer her up.

"Wanna play a game?" I ask.

"A game?"

"Yeah, you know, a contest. A competition. You've heard of games, right?"

"We might miss something. . . ."

"It's not a distracting game," I say. "Besides, if we don't do something to pass the time, I might hurl myself out the window."

"How do you play?"

"It's called Alphabetter," I explain. "The first person names something that makes them happy starting with *A*. Like, I might say 'aliens.' If I use the letter twice, I'll get an extra point, like if I say 'adorable aliens.' "

"Is that your real answer? Do adorable aliens make you happy?"

"Does this mean we're playing?"

"Yeah. Whatever," she says. "Why not?"

"Then that's my answer," I say. "Adorable aliens make me happy. Two points. Your turn."

"That's easy," she says. "Books make me happy."

"Okay, my tu—"

"Wait!" she cries. "*Brilliant* books. Brilliant . . . *brainy* books!"

It turns out Mellie is pretty good at Alphabetter. I find out she likes French foreign films (bleh) and hefty hippopotamuses (pretty cool). I tell her I like cream cheese, eclairs, and guacamole (but not together).

"Are you hungry?" asks Mellie when I choose meatballs for *M.*

"There you go detective-ing again," I say. I check the time on my phone. "Speaking of hungry, I've gotta get home for dinner. My mom will be home from the café any minute."

"I guess you'll never know my answer for *N,*" says Mellie, with a strange new expression on her face. It's a smile. A non-sarcastic, non-gloating smile.

"I don't know how I'll survive," I call over my shoulder as I rush out of the room.

I barrel down the two flights of stairs and out Mellie's front door, where I almost bump into the very last people I want to see at that moment—Harrison and his crew.

My first thought is that Mellie was right—Alphabetter *was* distracting. How the heck did we miss them during our stakeout?

My second thought is: *Oh no.*

Danica gasps. Ridley guffaws. Ben's eyebrows shoot up so far I think they might rocket right off his head. But Harrison doesn't react with alarm. He saunters over to me with his usual smirk, ready for another chance to trip me up. And I've literally walked right into this one.

CHAPTER 17

Brick

"Trex and Mellie sitting in a tree . . ." sing the kids of Hopewell Hill. A red-cheeked boy takes the lead, waving his arms like he's conducting an orchestra. I can't believe kids are still chanting that silly rhyme after all these years. Trex stands by the iron gate around Mellie's house, wriggling like a trapped bug, while they form a semicircle around him.

And me? I'm trespassing in someone's backyard, wedged between their trash bins so I can peep through a gap in the fence. Such glamorous work.

"Cut it out," says Trex. "We were working on a project. For school."

"Oh yeah?" says the red-cheeked kid.

"Yeah," says Trex. He thrusts his hands into his pockets, trying to look casual, but I notice the way he bites his lip and shifts from foot to foot. His charge is building. The iron fence is tugging at him.

"For which class?"

"Social studies."

"Likely story. You just don't want to admit that Mellie the Mouse is your girlfriend."

"She is not," says Trex, his face screwing into a grimace. "We got assigned to work together. It's not like I had any choice."

"Riiiight."

The chanting begins again: *Trex and Mellie sitting in a tree. K-I-S-S-I-N-G.*

Trex squirms, twisting his hips at an unnatural angle. That's when I spy a wisp of smoke rising from his pocket. He's positioned himself so the other kids can't see it, but it's right in my line of sight—a black-rimmed hole in the denim of his jeans that's growing wider and wider the longer he stands there.

"I'm not friends with Mellie the Mouse!" he shouts, the words so loud they reverberate in the air and silence the tittering kids around him. "I'd never hang out with her on purpose!"

He can't contain it any longer. Without removing his hands from his pockets, he uses his shoulders to ram past the kids. Once he clears them, he takes off in an unsteady jog toward his house. By now, the electricity in his body will be heating his blood.

He's agitated and nervous, which is only making it worse.

"What a freak," says the red-cheeked boy, and his audience nods.

"Yeah, what's his deal?" asks a blond girl.

"I always knew there was something weird about him," adds a boy in a tracksuit. "And to think he had such potential."

Normally, the cruelty of those children would heat my own blood and maybe send me storming across the street to give them a piece of my mind. But all I can think about is that smoke, wafting from Trex's concealed hand.

Because where there's smoke, there's bound to be fire.

CHAPTER 18

Mellie

I'm not friends with Mellie the Mouse! I'd never hang out with her on purpose!

Trex's words slice through the air like a blade. They rise all the way up to the third story of the tallest house on Hopewell Hill. Right into my window. Right into my ears. I can't say I'm surprised. Trex has proven before that he's just like the others. Aside from his lightning fingers, he's just another lemming, ready to follow Harrison off a cliff. Who needs a friend like that anyway?

After Trex runs off, the other kids wander away, chuckling about him. Did they just call him a "freak"? Did they say he was "weird"? Those words are normally reserved for me, and I feel a brief pang of satisfaction, hearing them hurled at the kid who just announced that he'd never be friends with me.

And then a rustling movement catches my eye. A

creeping figure emerges from Mr. Galleki's backyard—trench coat, baseball cap, dark glasses.

The Prowler!

I grab my phone and fumble for the camera app with jittery fingers. I won't be able to catch him red-handed, but at least I'll have evidence that he exists. My thumb jabs at the big red shutter button just as the screen goes black, and my heart sinks. I forgot to charge my phone while Trex was here, and now the battery is dead. A rookie mistake. A good detective never loses focus. And never ever lets her cell phone die.

The Prowler heads downhill, slinking in the shadows. He'll be out of view in a second, but if I hurry, I might be able to catch up with him outside and trail him from there. I burst out of my room and start down the stairs, almost colliding with Mother. She's carrying a glass of water up to my room.

"Mother . . . I can't. . . . I need to go. . . ."

"You can leave in just a minute," she says. "It's time to take your pill."

"But—"

"Let's go."

"Ugh," I grunt as I traipse back up the stairs to my room.

I shake one of the pink pills into the center of my palm, then drop it on my tongue. Mother hands me the glass, and I take a swig of water. Then I stick my tongue out at her. She searches the inside of my mouth while I say "ahhhh" like I'm at the dentist. She nods. Neither of us are enjoying this new role of hers, as warden of my medication, but Father insists.

As soon as she's gone, I dislodge the neon pill from the squishy recess under my tongue and drop it in the pocket of my hoodie, along with the others.

I move back to the window. Mr. Galleki is in his back-yard, dragging his trash cans out to the curb, but there's no sign of the Prowler now. I missed my chance. I stomp to my desk and flop into my chair to add today's sighting to my notes. When I'm done, I reach into my pocket and slowly count the growing collection of pills stashed there, slimy and coated with lint. Even though they're not in my belly, they've managed to ruin everything.

CHAPTER 19

Trex

Mellie hasn't spoken to me since the stakeout two days ago. I feel bad about what I said, about not being her friend. I feel even worse that she heard me say it. Now she refuses to look at me, let alone talk to me.

I have to admit, though, my life is easier without Mellie in it. I managed to salvage my reputation at school, sort of. I still hang out with Harrison's group, but I'm taking Mom's advice and keeping a low profile. So long as I laugh at their jokes and nod in agreement with everything they say, nobody pays much attention to me. And it's helping. My charge has been manageable. Sometimes I even forget I have one.

Plus, I haven't seen any trace of a so-called Prowler on Hopewell Hill. I let Mellie's talk about bad guys lurking in the shadows get into my head, but now I've come back to my senses. As I've been telling Mom for years, The Company isn't following us across the country. They're not trying to kidnap me and experiment on my brain. And we're not characters in a science fiction show—as awesome as it would be if we were.

"Hey, Dino-boy," says Harrison. I wince. We're at lunch, and I'm sticking to the plan and minding my own business. But the look on his face tells me that's about to change. "I dare you to steal Jumping Jackson's whistle." Coach Jackson, the basketball coach who monitors our lunch period, is standing at the cafeteria doors like a Roman sentry from a gladiator movie, with his arms crossed and a stony expression on his face.

"No way," I say. Stealing from a coach is definitely *not* the way to keep a low profile.

"Oh no," Harrison coos. "Widdle Twex doesn't want to get in twubble."

"Why don't *you* steal it?" I say.

"Been there, done that," says Harrison. He digs into his backpack and pulls out a red plastic whistle dangling from a vinyl rope. "It's a rite of passage around here. Anybody who's anybody steals the whistle."

"Is that true?" I ask, scanning the other faces.

"Yep," says Ben. "I did it last year."

"I've done it twice," Ridley boasts.

"It's no big deal," says Harrison. "Coach Jackson buys them in bulk. Every time a kid nabs one, he replaces it with a new color. All you have to do is swipe the whistle, then go to the stage and blow it. Everyone will cheer, and you'll be a rock star. You'll officially be one of us."

"Really?"

I search everyone's faces again. Nobody flinches. Then I glance over at Coach Jackson and assess the situation. Plastic whistle. No metal in the vicinity.

"Fine," I say. "I'll do it."

I know it's stupid, but I'm going to do it anyway. After the incident at Mellie's house, I have to prove myself. In order to blend in, apparently I have to blow a whistle in the middle of a crowded cafeteria. It sounds like opposite day, but this is middle school. Nothing makes sense.

I gather the remains of my lunch and walk slowly to the trash can. Jumping Jackson is stationed beside it, with the whistle tucked into the pocket of his loose athletic shorts. Its long string is trailing out. All I have to do is reach out and grab it. Easy. But first, balancing my tray in one hand, I stealthily touch the metal bar on one of the cafeteria chairs and release my charge. *Now* it's easy.

I drop my food wrappers into the bin and deposit my tray. I flex my fingers. My heart is thundering, but my charge is low. I can do this.

I reach for the string. My fingers find it, close around it, and pull. The material of Coach Jackson's shorts is so slippery, it practically delivers the whistle into my palm. He doesn't notice. The kids at my table give me thumbs-up signs and wave me toward the stage at the front of the room. I walk calmly up the steps and stand at center stage. A few kids notice, jabbing each other and pointing. I pucker my lips and blow.

The blare of the whistle echoes off the walls, and the cafeteria falls silent. Everyone stops talking and moving and even chewing. Every single head—I'm talking hundreds of heads—swivels in my direction. Coach Jackson storms over, his muscled chest heaving.

"What. Did. You. Just. Do?" he growls.

"I . . . um . . . did the prank," I stammer. "That . . . that everyone does."

"Nobody touches my whistle," he says through gritted teeth. "*Nobody*. Understand?"

"Yes, sir." And I do, finally, understand. I've been duped. I'm such an idiot.

Coach Jackson yanks the whistle away from me and then looks at his watch. "You've got twenty minutes left until the bell rings, Mr. Wilson. You're going to spend that time jumping."

That's when I realize that Jumping Jackson isn't named after his jump shot. He's named for his signature punishment. And everyone knows it but me. In the center of the cafeteria, Harrison, Ben, Danica, and Ridley are convulsing with laughter.

I do jumping jacks for twenty minutes straight. When the bell finally rings to release us from lunch, I stagger off the stage. The Hopewell Hill kids rush to meet me, still giggling.

I walk right past them.

CHAPTER 20

Mellie

Mrs. Blankenship, the school librarian, is usually immersed in a book when I walk in, but today she's watching the door, as if she's waiting for someone.

"Hi," I whisper, slipping quietly past her to my usual spot in the corner. It's lunchtime—time for me to pick up where I left off in the latest Myrtle Hardcastle mystery.

"Mellie," she calls after me. "Come here for a minute."

Uh-oh. The person she was waiting for was *me*? I double back and stand in front of her cluttered desk, fiddling with the straps of my backpack.

"I got a call from the principal today," she says. "She asked if a student had been spending the lunch period in the library."

"Uh . . . okay."

"When I told her you've been in here every day this year, she . . . she said she'd like you to spend your scheduled lunch hour in the cafeteria, with the other kids."

"But why?" I ask, at a volume bordering on inappropriate for the library. "What difference does it make to the principal where I sit for an hour?"

"I'm told the request came from . . . well, it came from your parents," she says, with guilt in her voice. As if she were the one banishing me from the library. Her eyes drop to the thick book on her desk, to avoid meeting mine.

"But—but that's not fair," I say. I sound childish and whiny, but the alternative to the library is . . . well, it's unthinkable. The cafeteria!

"I—I can't speak to that," says Mrs. Blankenship. "You'll have to talk to the principal. Or your parents. I'm sorry, Mellie."

I can tell she really *is* sorry, so I try not to take it out on her. Still, I let the door slam when I walk out. With slow, heavy footsteps, I trudge down the long corridor to the cafeteria. I imagine this is what walking to the executioner must feel like. Probably worse. My heart starts to thunder in my chest. Then my stomach joins the party, right on cue, gurgling and tossing. I plunge my hand into my pocket and find the unswallowed pills. I feel a quick twinge of regret for not taking them. I can feel the pressure in my abdomen building, like a balloon inflating—but a balloon studded with spikes. I bend forward slightly, to try to squish the pain, but that never works for long.

And then I notice something strange.

Even before I round the corner, I can tell that the cafeteria is quieter than usual. A low hum of chatter filters through the open double doors, but it should be a roar. I peer in and see that everyone is staring at the stage, some people pointing and laughing. My eyes instantly land on Harrison and company. How could I miss them, positioned in the middle of the cavernous room like they're the center of the universe? They're laughing hardest of all. I turn to see what's so funny.

It's Trex. He's onstage, doing jumping jacks. It's classic Coach Jackson, but I have a hunch Harrison is behind it. And my hunches are never wrong.

I slide into an empty table near the exit and hope nobody notices me. The mingled smells of everyone's lunches aren't helping my nausea. I keep my head down and nibble on the turkey sandwich Mother packed for me. I crumple up the smiley face Post-it she tucked in the brown paper bag. She can't expect to kick me out of the library and send me cutesy notes at the same time.

Eventually, the other kids get tired of watching Trex and return to their usual antics—tossing paper footballs, throwing food when the teachers aren't looking, or gathering around someone's phone to watch videos.

But I keep my eyes on Trex. What is he hiding? Why is the Prowler chasing him? What's his secret?

Ten minutes into his punishment, his face is splotchy and drawn. At the fifteen-minute mark, his jumping jacks are sloppy—his arms flopping around, his legs moving like they're weighted down. It's a far cry from the kid who pranced around the track like it was a leisurely stroll. What's different now?

I check my phone to see how much time is left in the lunch hour. Sure, Trex humiliated and rejected me, but that doesn't mean I want him to drop dead from too many jumping jacks. Trex only has two more minutes. He'll survive.

I slide my phone into my backpack, grateful I remembered to charge it today.

When the bell finally rings to release us from lunch, Trex looks like he wants to collapse, but he doesn't. He drags himself off the stage and brushes past the kids from Hopewell Hill. He looks defeated. Deflated.

Drained.

CHAPTER 21

Brick

Trex Wilson should've died.

The sky was angry on the night of the accident, lashing out at all the little people below. I took shelter in a depressing diner, ordered a black coffee, and sat on a rickety stool to wait out the storm. In some ways, I feel like I'm still waiting.

Nights like those were good for business. Accidents happen on nights like those. People get hurt. Which is exactly what we needed.

I'll never know what happened on that road. They said a driver going the opposite way lost control of his car, but he didn't live to tell the tale. The car Trex was riding in spun three times and crashed into a light pole. His father died at the scene, in the pouring rain, on the side of a four-lane highway. Trex and his mother were airlifted to the hospital, in critical condition. The boy sustained a serious head injury.

He should've died.

But their helicopter just happened to land at one of the most prominent research hospitals in the country. Not only did it have the best doctors and nurses on hand, it had something else. Something special. It had an affiliation with a multimillion-dollar corporation developing advanced medical technology—an organization known commonly as The Company.

And The Company had me.

Ronnie called me that night. "Where are you?"

"Um . . ." I looked around the diner and its lonely collection of misfits. "I don't think this place has a name."

"We found a candidate," she said. "A little boy. You should get over here."

I paid for my coffee and braved the sky's tantrum. I returned to the lab, where I met Trex Wilson for the first time. The boy who should've died but didn't.

And now, all these years later, my life is still tangled up with his. But he has no idea.

Yet.

CHAPTER 22

Mellie

I'm standing in a dark corner, tucked in behind the water fountain in an otherwise-empty hallway. All the other kids spilled out of school a while ago, but as usual, Trex hangs back. When he thinks the coast is clear, he pulls on his lucky baseball cap and trudges sullenly down the hall, where I'm waiting for him. A good detective knows how to make a dramatic entrance.

"I'm ready for a secret," I say. At the sound of my voice, Trex leaps into the air like a cartoon character who just sat on a tack.

"Are you trying to scare me to death?" he cries, clutching his chest. A bit melodramatic, if you ask me.

"You promised me a secret," I say. "I'd like to collect."

"Here's one," he says. "You're nuts."

"That's not a secret. Everybody knows that."

"Can't I just walk home in peace?"

"Sure," I say. "I guess that means you're not interested in the latest sighting of the Prowler."

"You're right," he says. "I'm not. The Prowler is a figment of your imagination. He's not real." But I catch a flicker of fear on his face.

"I saw him with my own eyes this time. He was in Mr. Galleki's backyard after the stakeout."

"That's not possible," says Trex. "We were . . . staking out. We would've seen him."

"He must've showed up just as you were leaving. I tried to take a picture of him, but my phone was dead."

"Whatever," says Trex. "I don't care."

"You'll care about this," I say, pacing in front of the sixth-grade lockers in the empty hallway, savoring this moment. The big reveal. "I had a revelation today." I hold up my phone like I'm presenting a piece of evidence at trial. "This."

"A phone?" he says wearily. "What does your phone have to do with the Prowler?"

"Nothing." I grin knowingly. "But it has everything to do with my other case. *The Mysterious Matter of Lightning Boy.*"

"Who's Light— Oh." He rolls his eyes. "Are you still stuck on that nonsense? I already told you—"

"The key to being a successful detective is to pay attention. And I've been paying attention. At the start of every day, you're a bundle of energy. By fifth period, you're dragging your feet. At the end of the day, you can hardly keep your eyes open. Until you put on your baseball cap."

"That's ridiculous."

"Is it? At track practice, you can run around and around without breaking a sweat. But today in the cafeteria, you were about to collapse because of a few jumping jacks. And I think it's because of this." I hold up my phone again.

"What are you suggesting? That I'm a cell phone?"

"Of course not," I say. "But kind of."

"That's the dumbest thing I've ever heard."

He refuses to meet my eyes, and I know I've hit the mark. Now to pull a confession out of him. "Are you . . . a robot?"

He sighs. "You've got to be kidding."

"Okay, fine, I haven't got all the details figured out yet. That's why I'd like to collect my secret."

"There is no secret!"

"My other guess is . . . well . . ." I can't believe I'm about to say this out loud. I usually rely on cold, hard evidence. But I can't rule out any possibilities at this point. "Are you . . . a superhero?"

"What?!"

"You heard me."

"I'm *definitely* not a superhero."

"I know," I say, my cheeks growing hot. "I didn't really think that."

"I'm just . . . ordinary," says Trex.

"We both know that's not true," I say. "My current theory is that the Prowler is after you because of your lightning or . . . whatever it is. If that's the case, I can help you. But only if you tell me what's going on."

He clamps his lips shut.

"I can keep a secret. I'm an expert at it, actually."

"But you told everyone that I shocked the statue!"

"I know, but that was before. If we're going to work together to catch the Prowler, we can't have any secrets. Not between the two of us." My hands are deep inside my pockets, fiddling with my stash of pills. A good detective never reveals *everything*.

Trex starts walking. Out of the school, into the withering heat of the parking lot. He plunges ahead, toward Hopewell Hill, without waiting for me. He wants to talk, I can tell. I catch up to him and silently fall into step beside him.

"It's static electricity," he says softly.

"Really?" I cry, a little too enthusiastically. I knew he was ready to crack, but sometimes even I'm amazed by my own skills. "But why? How?"

"I was in a car accident when I was little. The one that killed my father. I was injured so badly they thought I would die. I was declared brain-dead, in fact. I was airlifted to a big research hospital where they were working on experimental technology to replace damaged brain tissue. They were able to save my life, but . . . well . . . there were side effects."

"Like zapping people with your fingertips?"

"Exactly."

"So . . . you're not a robot, then? Or a superhero?"

"Nope. Just a kid with some artificial brain tissue."

"That's still really cool," I say. "Does it feel the same as having a normal brain?"

"How would I know?" he says. "I got the surgery when I was four. I don't remember what a 'normal' brain feels like."

"How does it work?"

"I don't really understand all of it. I know there's a battery that keeps it running. My implant has to be charged or else it goes dead. And, well . . . so do I."

"My grandpa has a pacemaker like that," I say.

"Mom disguised my charger so nobody would know when I was using it in public." He taps on his lucky baseball cap.

Then Trex stops and turns to me. Panic flashes in his eyes. "You won't tell anyone, will you? Mom would kill me if she knew I told you."

"I promise," I say.

"Swear?"

"Of course. I'd make it a pinkie-swear, but I'm afraid you'd burn my finger."

Trex gives me a groggy, halfway smile. "I can't believe it," he says. "Mellie Chandler just cracked another joke."

Trex

Mellie Chandler knows everything. It isn't the worst thing that could've happened, but it's close. Probably in the top five. One thing is for sure now—I'm stuck with her.

"So who's the Prowler?" she asks, hovering next to me like a shadow.

"Beats me," I say. "Probably some goon hired by the company that made my implant."

"Why would they be chasing you? Did you stiff them on your medical bills or something?"

"Kinda. You see, the stuff in my brain is valuable. Like, *really* valuable. The Company had been developing the technology for years, but it didn't work until I came along. They wanted to use me as a test case, but Mom said no. She didn't want that kind of life for me. But The Company said my brain was their property, and they could do what they wanted with me. So we took off in the middle of the night, and we've been running ever since. Every time Mom gets spooked, we pack up and leave."

"Whoa," breathes Mellie. "That sounds like . . ."

"A movie?"

"I was going to say book, but close enough."

We've reached the garden. The statue peers down at us with what looks like concern. An old man is seated on the bench in front of her. He's gray-haired and stooped and squinting at a paper map. I didn't even know they still made those. When he sees us, he rises with difficulty. "Excuse me," he asks, taking shambling steps toward us. "Can you kids direct me to Colorado Street?"

"It's that way," I say, pointing down the hill. "Two blocks away."

"Ah, excellent," he says. "There's a house for sale on Colorado. My wife and I are considering making an offer. Ruthie's sick of the cold weather. Now that our kids are grown, she'd like to bask in the sun, you know?"

I nod, trying to be polite. Beside me, I feel Mellie clam up, about to go full roly-poly. She just stares at him, stupefied.

"The name's Mack," he says. He comes closer, extending his hand. Now Mellie and I both stiffen, blinking at him like aliens who have never seen a handshake before. I don't have much of a charge at the moment, but I don't want to risk it. He's old. What if I shock him and he has a heart attack or something? Eventually, he pulls his hand back and scratches at the wispy hairs on his balding head. "Hey, do you kids like cookies?" he asks, ignoring our snub and picking up a Tupperware from the bench. "Ruthie makes a mean snickerdoodle. She sent me over here with a batch of them for the realtor, but I have to admit, I snuck one or two on the drive over. I'll trade you guys some cookies for the inside scoop on the neighborhood."

Mellie catches my eye and shakes her head. "No thanks," I say, even though the cookies look pillowy and sugary and delicious. "We don't want to spoil our dinner."

"Of course," says Mack. "Well, it sure was a pleasure meeting you kids. Maybe we'll be neighbors soon. What did you say your names were?"

"Ridley," Mellie blurts out, suddenly finding her voice. "I'm Ridley Duncan. And this is Harrison Palmer."

I shoot her a look that says: *Huh?*

She shoots me one back that says: *Hush.*

"Thanks again," says Mack.

As he turns to go, his loafer bumps the raised edge of the sidewalk. Suddenly, he's toppling over like a tree, his face heading straight for the concrete, his feeble old limbs powerless to stop it. I'm standing directly in his path. I can catch him. But instead, my body moves on autopilot, like it's been taught. No contact, ever. I leap out of the way.

Mellie, on the other hand, drops the books in her arms and swoops in between us. She places her palms on Mack's chest, holding him upright with a grunt. I don't even step in to help as she struggles under his weight. It all happens so quickly, and I just stand there, useless.

Mack recovers his balance, clutching Mellie's arm. He thanks her repeatedly and offers her cookies again. He won't even look at me.

"Good luck with the house hunt," I mumble, my face burning red.

"Hmph," he snorts at me, stalking off. I can only imagine what he'll report back to Ruthie about the jerks on Hopewell Hill.

"There's something off about that guy," says Mellie as we watch him disappear down the hill. "I don't trust him."

"Are you serious?" I say. "He was a nice old man. And I almost let him eat concrete. *I'm* the one who can't be trusted."

"You did the right thing," says Mellie. "You could've hurt him with your . . . side effect."

"Whatever," I grumble. "I might as well turn myself over to The Company. I'd rather be a guinea pig than . . . this." I look down at my own hands with disgust.

"Don't say that," says Mellie.

"Uh-oh," says a familiar voice. "Are you two having a little lover's spat?"

We turn around to face the *real* Harrison Palmer sauntering into the garden, surrounded by his loyal troop of followers. I can tell by the look on his face that this is not going to end well.

CHAPTER 23

Mellie

Splash.

That's me hitting the water. Going under. As soon as we spot Harrison and his friends in the garden, I'm right back in that dunk tank. The first pang squeezes my stomach like a vise as he struts over to us. My face goes hot and stinging. My throat starts to close.

"We were wondering why we never see you two walking home," Harrison says. "Now we know. It's because you're in the garden making out." He does a gross lip-smacking noise that makes me want to vomit. My stomach rumbles so loud I wonder if anyone can hear it.

"We're working on a project," says Trex. "I told you."

"Oh, right," says Harrison. "A 'project.' Why don't you guys take a break from your 'project' and hang out with us for a little while?"

"It's due tomorrow," says Trex.

"Oh, come on," says Ben, hopping along the sidewalk on some imaginary hopscotch board. "Live a little."

"We thought we'd pick up where we left off at lunch," says Harrison. "With a little game of truth or dare." The very idea makes Danica erupt in giggles.

"We can't," says Trex. "We really need to—"

"Buckaw!" clucks Harrison.

At that, Trex's jaw tenses, and the cramp tightens in my belly. I know Trex's brain doesn't allow him to read minds, but I'm desperate. "Don't do this," I try to tell him telepathically. "Harrison isn't worth it." I study his face— his eyes steel, his lips a grim line. He can't hear me. And he's not going to let Harrison's "buckaw" go unanswered.

"It makes sense you'd be scared," taunts Harrison, "after that fiasco at lunch today."

"You set me up!" says Trex.

"It was a harmless prank," says Harrison. "Don't be so touchy."

Harrison and Trex hold each other's stares like gun-slingers about to duel. "Fine," says Trex. "Let's play."

Ridley grins and says something in my direction, but her voice is muffled. I'm fully submerged now. I'm watching the scene unfold before me, but I'm not really here. I'm behind Plexiglas. I'm gasping for air. I put my hands deep in my pockets so I can cradle my stomach without anybody noticing. My fingers land on the pills, and I desperately wish that I'd taken one that morning. Instead, I start counting them. *One-two-three-four-*

five . . . It doesn't make the pain stop, but at least it distracts me.

"Truth or dare?" asks Harrison.

"Truth," says Trex.

Harrison scratches his chin and stares into the distance, like he's thinking hard about what he's going to ask. But he has his question holstered and ready. That's why he challenged Trex in the first place. He knows what he's doing.

"Are you and Mellie the Mouse . . . friends?" he asks. His words are blurry, the way voices sound underwater, but I know what he's trying to do. He's trying to get Trex to say it again, right in front of me.

I'm not friends with Mellie the Mouse! I'd never hang out with her on purpose!

The gurgle in my stomach becomes a full-blown eruption. I scrunch over slightly, to cut the pain. Everyone is focused on Trex, so I take small, shuffling steps backward. I gaze up at my bedroom window above us. My room is so close—so dark and safe and empty. Maybe I can sneak away without anyone noticing.

"Yes," says Trex. His answer is clear and sharp. It cuts through the barrier of Plexiglas and water. Otherwise, I'd be certain I heard him wrong.

"I knew it," says Harrison triumphantly. The others chuckle and wrinkle their noses, as if he revealed he still wets the bed. "It's a real shame, Trex. You could've been cool."

"Truth or dare?" asks Trex, still steely-eyed. Rolling his hands into fists.

"Dare," smirks Harrison.

Trex pauses. He hasn't thought this far ahead. He doesn't have a humiliation at the ready, like Harrison did.

But I do. My stomach still hurts, but I shuffle over to Trex. I tug on his sleeve and whisper into his ear. The perfect dare.

"Well?" says Harrison.

"I dare you to climb the statue of the Unnamed Girl," says Trex.

Harrison laughs and tries to sound laid-back, but he can't conceal his nerves. Not from me. "Are you sure you want to waste your dare on this?" he asks. "Climbing the statue is so last summer. Why don't you give me a real challenge?"

"I'd like to see you repeat your famous climb," says Trex.

"Suit yourself." Harrison shrugs, but his cheeks have already begun to glow.

We gather around the base of the statue as Harrison hoists himself onto the platform. He stacks his feet on the boots of the Unnamed Girl, the way little kids do when they're dancing with their parents. He easily scales the lower folds of her skirt. When he reaches her waist, he grins down at us, his trademark confidence returning. He looks up at the girl's upraised arm, and I can tell he's doing the calculations in his head. If he can fling himself onto her arm, he can easily pull himself the rest of the way. But I have math class with Harrison. I know calculations aren't his strong suit.

"He's going for it!" whispers Ridley.

We hold our collective breath as Harrison's left arm releases the girl's torso and strikes out on its own. With a grunt, he thrusts himself into the air. His fingertips graze the statue's bronze bicep. But he can't hold on.

He shrieks as he falls.

We all do.

Trex

For the second time today, I'm the only thing between someone's skull and the hard ground. I've spent a lifetime training myself to keep my distance from people. But I push all that aside. I won't be a useless bystander this time, not even for Harrison Palmer. I throw my arms open wide, which is completely pointless because there's no way I can actually catch him as he falls. But that doesn't occur to me until it's too late.

Harrison lands on me with an "oof." My legs give out under me, and I crumple onto the platform. I'm flat on my back with the wind knocked out of me and a squirming Harrison on top of me. We're a tangle of arms and legs, but at least all those limbs are still moving. No broken bones. No twisted ankles. Slowly, we pick ourselves up.

"What the heck was that?" yelps Harrison.

"Huh?"

"You heard me. What was *that*?"

"I think you mean 'Thanks for catching me,'" I say between panting breaths.

"No thanks if you electrocute me in the process," snarls Harrison. He hops off the platform, where his concerned friends surround him like bodyguards.

"I don't know what you're talking about," I say. I hear the tremble in my own voice. I hope nobody else does.

"You zapped me!" yells Harrison.

"No, I didn't." I stuff my hands in my pockets and flex my fingers, trying to shake off the tingling feeling still vibrating through them. I *did* shock Harrison, lightly, but that should be the end of it. My charge should've dissipated by now. Why can I still feel it? Why is it so strong?

"Yes you did!" says Harrison. "Just like the Mouse said."

"Why do you always have to be such a jerk?" I grumble. "I was trying to help you."

"Excuse me?" says Harrison, pushing through his pack of bodyguards to face me. "What did you just call me?"

"You heard."

Before I can react, he charges at me. But he's not as dumb as I thought. He avoids my skin altogether. Instead, he reaches up and swipes my baseball cap.

"Give that back!" I cry.

"Come get it," he says, holding it over his head. I remove my hands from my pockets and lunge for the hat, but Harrison ducks under my arm. When I whirl around, he's standing beside the statue, grinning, spinning my lucky cap on his fingertip.

"What's with this hat anyway?" he asks, examining it. "Why are you so attached to this ugly thing?"

"Give. That. Back!"

"Make me. Freak!"

I go after him again, and he chucks the hat into the air as high as he can. It hits its mark, catching one of the fingertips of the Unnamed Girl. Dangling six feet over my head.

I roar. Harrison must realize he's pushed it too far, because he stumbles away from me, backing toward the statue. I follow. I charge for him.

A bolt of bright blue light zigzags between us.

Harrison cries out in pain.

Mellie

"Trex?"

"Leave me alone."

We're alone in the garden now because everyone else

ran off screaming. Trex's secret is definitely not a secret anymore. His hat is swinging gently from the Unnamed Girl's outstretched fingers.

"Harrison will be fine," I say. "Besides, he deserved it."

He stares down at his hands, opening and closing his fists like they belong to someone else. "Something's going on. The shocks were never like this before. They were harmless little zaps, not lightning bolts. What if I really hurt someone, Mellie?"

"You should try talking to your mom," I say. "She might surprise you."

"Hmph," snorts Trex. "As soon as Mom hears about this, it's all over. We'll be packed up and gone by tomorrow. Unless I get arrested first."

"Harrison may be a weasel, but he's not a snitch. Maybe your mom won't find out about this."

"Whatever," he mumbles. "What's the use in staying here anyway if I'm the local freak?"

"As the current local freak, I can assure you it's not that bad," I say, grinning.

He doesn't respond.

"Hello? Mellie Chandler just cracked a joke. . . ."

"Yeah," he mumbles. "Whatever."

"All right, that's it." I let my backpack slide off my shoulders and set my books down. "I'm going up!"

Trex lifts his drooping head and opens his mouth to protest, but I'm already on the platform. "You saw what just happened to Harrison," he says. "I can't let you do this."

"Harrison is a fraud," I say over my shoulder. "I've got this." I have no reason to believe the truth of that statement, given my overall clumsiness and lack of interest in pointless physical activity. But it sounds convincing. I ascend the lower folds of the skirt slowly and painfully. After several long, excruciating minutes, I make it to the spot where Harrison attempted his ill-fated leap.

"Are you okay?" calls Trex. I almost peer down at him, but I don't need a reminder of how high up I am. Or how far I have to fall.

"I'm. Just. Great," I grunt. I'm drenched in sweat, clasping the statue in a bear hug, and afraid to move too much for fear of sliding off it like butter off a hot pan. Just great.

"I'll find a ladder," Trex yells from below me. "We can get the hat some other way!"

"I can do this!" I say. I decide against leaping into thin air like Harrison did. Instead, I hold on tight and keep shinnying up, inch by inch. I eventually make it to her shoulder. Then to eye level. Up close, she isn't stern at all. She is fierce. I wrap myself around her arm, upside down like a frightened monkey, and edge along it. It feels endlessly long. When I reach her elbow, I stretch my own arm, imagining it's made of elastic. I close my eyes. My fingertips brush against something fabric. Then it's gone.

"You did it!" cries Trex. "You did it, Mellie!"

I open my eyes, and the Unnamed Girl is empty-handed. I whoop with glee. Against my better judgment, I look down to see Trex place the so-called "lucky" hat back on his head. And that's when I lose my grip. I shriek and scramble to regain my hold on the statue's arm, but in the process, my legs swing free. I'm hanging on by my sweaty palms now, which are growing slicker by the second. I can't hold on. The only thing below me—*way* below me—is a solid wooden platform.

Then, suddenly, Trex is there, too. "I'll catch you," he says, spreading his arms wide. "You can let go."

"But . . . I'll crush you."

"Not as much as Harrison did."

"You'll shock me!"

"Yep."

"Will it hurt?"

"Yep. But not as much as a broken bone."

I squeeze my eyes shut as gravity does its work and pulls me down. I land awkwardly on Trex, in a sort of half catch, with his hands under my armpits. The shock isn't so different from what I'm used to—like the sting of cold water. It hurts for a second, and then it's gone. And I'm on solid ground.

"Thank you," he says. "But you're nuts, you know."

"Yeah," I say. "So I've been told."

CHAPTER 24

Brick

Static electricity was always a problem. Our technology was so sensitive that even the smallest jolt would short it out. It's like what happens to TVs and computers when a house gets struck by lightning. Now imagine that happening to someone's brain. Not good, right? So we developed safeguards to channel those electrons away from our machinery and out the subject's fingertips. Call me crazy, but an annoying little jolt seems like a far better alternative than, say . . . dying.

Years ago, when I told Ronnie about the side effect, her eyes welled up with tears. "Imagine going your whole life never able to touch anyone," she whimpered.

"Meh," I said. "I wouldn't mind it."

"You're stone-cold," she said.

And maybe she was right. I didn't have time to get all emotional about my work. I was too busy trying to change the world, one brain at a time. So what if there were a few hiccups?

Allan, for example.

Long before Trex, there was Allan, a bird-watcher from Winnemucca, Nevada. Allan was dying.

He volunteered to get the implant back when we were still working out the kinks. He'd already been diagnosed with an incurable brain disease, so what did he have to lose? The doctors had given him months to live, at best. The Company threw a huge party for him before the procedure, as if he were going into space. And he *was* heading into unchartered territory, forging a path for others to follow. Or so we hoped. When Allan didn't die during surgery, we threw him an even bigger party, just for surviving. The public relations guys were ecstatic. The scientists even more so.

Allan lasted three glorious months. Twice as long as anyone else.

Nobody ever figured out what happened to him. He just keeled over one day on a nature walk, in the middle of nowhere. The coroner found burn marks on his skin, and some people guessed he'd been struck by lightning. But it wasn't raining that day. The official cause of death was ruled a heart attack (with some persuasion from The Company, I'm sure). But a forensic analysis showed that the hardware in his brain was fried. Allan's machinery had failed. But why?

Allan's death was bad for morale. Everyone on

the team felt like they had blood on their hands, even though Allan knew the risks. Even though he would've cashed in his chips one way or another. Nobody wanted to try again right away. Except me. And Dr. Vogel, of course. That's how I got my nickname. Not because I'm strong (even though I am), but because I'm solid. Unshakable, even when things go wrong. Content to be a useful chunk in a larger structure.

So I pressed ahead, spurred on by Dr. Vogel, who taught me that meaningful progress requires sacrifice. We'd learn from Allan's death and use that knowledge to develop a better product. It may sound cold, but the magnitude of what we were building was worth the cost. An implant that would bridge the gap between man and machine. Technology that would fuse biological material with metal, plastic, and electricity to create a new organ. A better one.

We could improve lives. We could *save* them.

If we lost a patient or two? That was simply the price of a better world.

And here we are, a decade after Allan's death, and we still haven't made sense of it. Ronnie sends me the files—hundreds of them. There were formal inquiries, studies, investigations, committees. All of them were inconclusive.

Not a single one mentions lightning.

CHAPTER 25

Trex

I'm curled up between Barnaby and Mom on the sofa, wrapped in my annoying rubber blanket. The TV is on, but all I can think about is the look on Harrison's face when I shocked him. And the shrieks and jeers of the other kids. And that word they used over and over: *"Freak."*

Maybe they're right. Maybe I *am* a freak. I thought Mom and her fear of The Company were the only things preventing me from a normal life, but maybe I'm just not cut out for normal. I can't control my charge anymore, despite the rubber blankets and secret bits of metal stashed in my pockets. I'm a public hazard. Maybe The Company *should* cage me up like a lab rat.

And what if my growing power is a sign of something worse? What if the charge is increasing because my equipment is malfunctioning? Mom always told me my brain makes me less—not more—vulnerable to the things that attack a body. She said The Company installed backups and fail-safes to make sure I never have an outage. That the technology will last longer than I will. That my artificial synapses will be firing long after my heart stops beating. But maybe she only says this to make us both feel better. Because we both know that technology is as fragile as flesh—and just as unpredictable.

"Mom?" I whisper.

Her eyelids flutter like I've startled her out of a dream.

"Mom? Are you all right?"

"Sorry, Trex, I'm just exhausted. Francie called out sick today, so I had to cover her tables at the café. I didn't even get my lousy twenty-minute break. Is everything okay?"

"Yeah, it's just . . . can I ask you something?"

"Of course, Trex. Anything."

"It's about the side effects."

"Oh." She sits up straighter. "Has something happened?"

"No." Nothing except almost frying Harrison Palmer to a crisp in front of all his friends. "It's just that the shocks have been a little . . . stronger lately."

"Really?" She's sitting bolt upright now. "Has anyone noticed?"

"No." Except all the middle schoolers who think I'm a freak and might show up at any moment with torches and pitchforks.

"Have you been following the rules?"

"Yes."

"What about your moods?" she asks, rising from the couch. "Have you been getting upset? Scared? Angry?"

"Maybe a little," I say. The understatement of the century.

"You're about to hit puberty, Trex, so that's an added complication." The p-word coming out of Mom's mouth makes me cringe. She goes to the bookshelf and removes a thick textbook called *Circuit Analysis for Beginners.* Three towns ago, Mom took a class at the local community college to learn what she could about my technology. So she could help me if anything went wrong. "The weather is also making things worse. Dry air increases static electricity."

"So it's normal that the shocks are getting stronger?" I ask.

"Maybe," she says, flipping through the book. "But I'm no scientist. If you're worried, then—"

"I don't want to leave!" I blurt out. Even though I've gone from "intriguing new kid" to "freak" in record time, I still want to give Hopewell Hill a chance. I'm not ready to throw in the towel yet. "I was just wondering . . ."

"I know what you're thinking," says Mom, "and it's out of the question."

"It's been eight years, Mom. If we could just talk to someone at The Company . . ."

"The moment they find us, it's over. Do you want to spend the rest of your life in a lab?"

"You can't be serious. . . ."

"Trex," she says, in a tone both weary and not-having-it, "you've lived a sheltered life because of your condition. You don't know how awful people can be. How greedy."

"That's not true!" I shoot back. "I've seen *E.T.* six times! Every bad guy in every science fiction movie wants to capture the alien or the kid with 'abilities' and do experiments on him. But that only happens in movies, Mom. This is real life!"

"This is not up for discussion. Do you hear me?"

"It isn't fair!"

"*Fair?*" she fires back. "Do you think any of this is fair to me? Do you think I intended to spend my life moving from town to town, running away from my past like a criminal? I've done all of this for *you*! I haven't spent the last eight years keeping you safe only to let you run right into the arms of those madmen!"

"None of that is about me!" I shout. "It's you being paranoid. It's your fault I never went to school or had any friends or had a real home! It's your fault I'm a freak!" I hop up from the couch, letting my rubber blanket slump to the floor. Barnaby darts to the other side of the room.

A soft buzzing starts vibrating behind my ears, like a mosquito circling my head. Only the mosquito is *in* my head somehow. That's new. But this definitely isn't the time to bring up another pesky brain issue. I shake it off, and it recedes into the background.

"You are so ungrateful!" Mom yells, slamming her heavy book shut. "Go to your room!"

"You are so mean!" I shout.

I throw up my hands in exasperation, and a fizzing trail of blue leaps from my fingertips to the lamp beside me. The sharp pop makes Mom scream and Barnaby whimper. A burst of sparks and glass rises up over the lampshade like a Roman candle. Then everything goes dark.

Now she knows what I mean by stronger shocks.

The buzzing in my head stops, and everything grows eerily quiet. I can't see Mom's face, but I can tell by the sound of her voice what it must look like.

"Pack your things," she says. "We're leaving in the morning."

CHAPTER 26

Mellie

I'm hunched over my social studies homework—I really *do* have a project due tomorrow—when Mother knocks on my bedroom door. She pokes her head inside.

"What are you working on?" she asks.

"Social studies," I sigh. "Who knew ancient Mesopotamia could be so boring?"

"Probably most people."

"Yeah, I guess you're right."

"You came home late today," she says. "What were you up to after school?"

A series of images flash through my head—Harrison falling, Trex shocking him, looking into the eyes of the Unnamed Girl. "Just . . . hanging out in the garden," I say.

"You've been making friends this year," says Mother. "We're thrilled to see that."

"Yeah," I mumble. "Now the neighbors won't think you keep me locked in the attic."

Mother ignores my snide remark. "You seem happy," she says.

"Oh." I glance out the window. For the first time in as long as I can remember, maybe I *am* happy. Or as close as I can get. Even the Unnamed Girl seems happier this afternoon, or perhaps it's the way the light is hitting her.

"You know, Dad and I just want you to get better," says Mother. "We're only trying to help. I hope you understand that."

Something in her tone makes me twist around in my seat and look at her. She's standing in the doorway, fidgeting with something. It's a clear plastic cup with a red twist-on lid, the kind you only see in doctor's offices. She looks down at it when I do, as if seeing it for the first time. "We can't help you unless we know what's going on . . ." Her voice is already apologetic.

"What's that for?"

"It's standard practice," says Mother, turning the cup over in her hands. "Dr. Colson does this for lots of his patients."

"He does *what*?" I ask with a screechy voice. I know what she's getting at, but I'm going to make her say it.

"Um, testing. Urine testing. To make sure you're taking your pills."

"Dr. Colson agreed to this?" I ask.

"I spoke to his receptionist," she says. "She said their office often provides drug testing."

"For addicts!" I snap. "Not for kids who forget to take their pills." I long to reach into my pocket to feel them there, but I don't dare risk it.

Hot tears bloom in the corners of my eyes. I'm not sure whether I'm sad or angry or humiliated, or all three. "I won't do it!" I say.

"Mellie, don't make this difficult," says Mother, chewing on the side of her lip.

"Please, Mom." I never call her that, and it feels weird. But right now, I need her to be Mom. "I'll read the brochure, I promise."

"You already promised," she says. "You said you'd take your pills. You lied to us."

"Mom—"

"We're trying to help you get better, Mellie. But we need you to cooperate."

"We?" I shoot back, glaring at her.

Her brow bunches up into a cluster of wrinkles. She looks anguished, like someone who just stubbed her toe but refuses to cry out. "You're not allowed to leave this house until you give me a sample. We have to do this until we know we can trust you." The words come out of her mouth, but they're Father's words, I can tell.

"Mom, don't do this."

"I'm going to Dr. Colson's office tomorrow morning,

so I need it by then," says Mother. She moves closer, holding the cup out to me, but I don't take it. It hangs there in the space between us. "Mellie, please."

She places it on my desk, next to my social studies book. Then she slips quietly out of the room. The tears spill out of my eyes, and the words I'm supposed to be reading blur together.

In my head, I silently start making a list.

Amethysts.

Balloon animals.

Chocolate chip cookies. Three points.

I'm all the way to *K* when there's movement outside my window. Unfortunately, it's only Harrison. He's walking by with a bounce in his step, stuffing something into his mouth and scattering crumbs all over the sidewalk. I swipe the tears from my cheeks and pick up my binoculars for a better view. He's eating cookies. Snickerdoodles. I guess he's recovered from his run-in with Trex.

I have a feeling Trex hasn't fared quite so well.

Him and me both.

CHAPTER 27

Trex

The open cardboard box is like a deep, dark canyon. I drop in a teddy bear wearing overalls, from that time we went to a carnival somewhere in Oklahoma. I can't remember which city, but it doesn't matter. The box swallows him up regardless.

"How's it going?" asks Mom, stepping cautiously into the room. It's been twenty minutes, and I've packed four T-shirts and one stuffed bear.

"Fine," I mumble, though I don't feel remotely fine.

She sighs and stands beside me. We both stare into the mostly empty box. "I know you want to stay here, Trex, but it's too risky. Hopewell isn't the place for us. But that doesn't mean there isn't one. Once we figure out what's going on with you, we'll find somewhere else to settle down. Me and you. I promise."

I grunt in response. I've heard it all before.

"Have you thought about where you want to go next?" she asks. "We can go anywhere you want . . . beaches, mountains. It's totally up to you."

"Whatever. I don't care."

Mom pushes a strand of hair out of my eyes. She's still not afraid to touch me, no matter how many times I shock her. Or destroy light fixtures. "I was thinking somewhere down south. Somewhere sunny, but without all this dry heat. Maybe Florida?"

"Yeah," I say, with as little enthusiasm as possible. "Sounds great."

"I wanted this to work out," she says. "I really did. Just . . . don't give up on me, Trex. Okay?"

I don't answer.

She sighs again. "I need to run to the café in a few minutes. I have to turn in my uniform and pick up my last paycheck. That'll help us get started in . . . wherever we end up."

I still don't answer, and she finally leaves.

As soon as she does, the buzzing starts again. At first, I try to ignore it. It's annoying, but it went away last time, so I'm sure it'll eventually stop.

Instead, it gets louder. More shrill, with a metallic sort of rattle. I stick a finger in each ear, to block the sound, but that only makes it echo. The sound is *in* there. What is going on?

Suddenly, a blinding white light flashes behind my eyes, so bright it stings. It only lasts for a moment, but it disorients me, and I stumble backward into the stack of boxes Mom always keeps on hand. I steady them before they topple over. I don't want Mom to hear the commotion and come running back in. It's just a glitch. It's nothing to worry about. She'll only panic and make everything worse.

But then everything gets worse, even without her help. It feels like a thousand needles stabbing the soft tissue of my brain. I've never experienced anything like this. It's horrendous. Unbearable. It . . . hurts.

I'm in physical pain. I've never been in pain before— at least not that I can remember.

Now I've got something to worry about.

CHAPTER 28

Brick

Trex has always been a fighter. Even when he was unconscious, when they laid his limp body out on the operating table, I could tell. Behind those closed eyelids, he was struggling to stay alive. I knew he was the one, that he'd be our success story. When he recovered, he'd be as good as new. In fact, he'd be better than new.

When the surgeries were over, I volunteered for the overnight shift to monitor his progress. Everyone else had families at home, but not me. What did I care about staying up all night? The lab was my home. Ronnie was my only friend (if you could call her that). And the boy was my crowning achievement. I had to make sure he lived. So I sat beside his bed, night after night, listening to the beeping and wheezing machines.

One night, I discovered a plastic bag tucked into a drawer, containing everything that had been salvaged from the scene of the accident—toys, sunglasses, a wallet. And the clothes the boy had been wearing—or what remained of them. They'd cut his T-shirt off in the emergency room, so it had a jagged slice down the center. I held it up in the dim light of the lab. It was impossibly tiny. It reminded me how small he was, how very young, and I prayed he'd stay asleep until morning. So his first vision on waking up wouldn't be me.

On the front of the shirt, cut in two, was a picture of a dinosaur in mid-roar. A single word was still intact in the corner.

"T. rex."

CHAPTER 29

Mellie

My bladder is full, but I refuse to go to the bathroom. I glare at the stupid plastic cup and turn up my music—my moodiest mix of classical concertos. Mellie Chandler will not give in that easily. As if house arrest is any kind of punishment for a shut-in anyway.

But I still can't concentrate on ancient Mesopotamia, so I roll my chair over to the window. It's early evening, and the world outside is quiet. Parents are home from work; kids have been called inside for dinner. But the neighborhood is not without clues. For example, Mr. Galleki's trash bins are still on the curb, which means he hasn't been home since trash day to drag them inside.

Speaking of Mr. Galleki's backyard, it's the last known location of the Prowler, and I still haven't searched the scene. I use my binoculars to peer over the fence. A hose, some chew toys, and—ugh—a few calling cards from Walter, Ms. Lewis's yappy dog. And . . . something shiny.

It winks up at me, pressed into the dirt where the trash bins normally go. It's probably a stray piece of garbage that fell out of a bag. Probably tinfoil or cellophane, a candy wrapper or a scrap of wrapping paper. But a good detective is never content with "probably." I grab my notebook and my backpack and bolt toward the bedroom door, but then I remember. I'm grounded.

I pace the length of my room. The one time I want to leave the house, and I'm not allowed. This shiny object could be the breakthrough I've been waiting for—it could be the key that unlocks the mystery of The Company *and* Trex's brain, all at once. I can't just leave it lying there. I can't let this opportunity pass me by.

I tug on my favorite hoodie over my penguin-print pajamas. I connect my phone to the speakers and turn the music up as loud as it will go, blaring the angsty concertos. If my parents hear it, they'll think I'm still here, fuming, and they'll leave me alone.

I'll be back in my room before anyone notices I'm gone.

Trex

I'm no longer in my room. A millisecond ago, I was fumbling for the door, racked by intense pain. I was just about to cave in and cry out for Mom when the headache suddenly stopped. And then the weirdest thing happened.

Now I'm standing in a field. Literally. I'm surrounded by rolling hills and a surreal blue sky. In the distance, I can make out a village with a fire pit in the center, ringed by small, rickety houses with thatched roofs. Beyond that, a marble palace shimmers in the distance.

I recognize this place. I'm in Oren, the kingdom from *Legends of Oren*. The *fictional* kingdom from *Legends of Oren*.

Am I hallucinating? Am I dead?

Is heaven . . . a video game?

A trumpet blares from somewhere behind me, and the ground begins to shake. Before I turn around, I know it's the Peasants' Army, riding in from the valley to overthrow the evil king. The horses are upon me before I can flee, but the herd parts down the center to avoid me, like water rushing past a stone. The men charging by wear rags and carry dented shields. I hear their individual voices shouting "huzzah" as they pass. I distinguish their features—twisted with fear, anger, and vengeance. I smell their sweat, the kicked-up grass, the horses' bodies. It feels so real. But it can't be.

I reach out to one of the animals, to run my hand along its dark haunches. The impact, at that speed, should wound me, crush the delicate bones in my hand. But I'm unscathed. My hand moves right through the horse. Or the horse moves through me.

What is happening to me?

Overhead, a dragon with translucent green scales swoops through the impossibly blue sky.

Mellie

I scamper across the street and quietly slip into Mr. Galleki's backyard. Who knew breaking and entering would be so easy? But I still have to be on my guard. If the Prowler was here once, he might come back, especially if he left a clue lying around.

I'm scanning the ground for the item that caught my eye, focusing on the patch of half-dead grass where the garbage cans normally go, when I hear a grumbling sound from the other side of the fence. Like wheels rumbling over asphalt. Like someone dragging huge trash bins in from the curb. Uh-oh.

I dart into a corner and stand perfectly still, holding my breath. My heart is thrumming wildly, but my stomach is surprisingly calm. Even though I'm about to get caught trespassing in my penguin jammies, I don't feel panicked. I feel alive.

Ms. Lewis arrives at the gate and frowns when she notices it's open, but she doesn't dwell on it. She maneuvers the bins back into place and returns to the house. She doesn't see me. I exhale in relief, until I realize I am no longer alone in the yard.

Walter the Yorkie stares up at me with suspicious, beady eyes. He cocks his head and clamps down hard on the object in his mouth, as if he's afraid I'll steal it. Which, of course, I intend to, because he's found the shiny thing.

"Shhhh!" I whisper, pressing a finger to my lips. "C'mon, Walter, hand it over!"

I step slowly toward the dog, holding up my hands to show him I mean no harm. But he braces himself and growls, protecting his new treasure. The only thing preventing an eruption of yappy barks is the shimmering red item in his mouth. I slowly and quietly unlatch the gate again, letting it swing open. Walter thinks he's won, that he's scared me off with his ferocious snarl.

"Sorry," I whisper to him. "I need this more than you do."

In one swift movement, I yank the object out of the dog's mouth and sprint out of the yard. Walter chases me for a moment and then doubles back, running in frantic circles in front of Mr. Galleki's house, barking so loud and hysterically that Ms. Lewis bursts out the front door. I hear a few other doors creak open behind me as my annoyed neighbors join Ms. Lewis outside to see what the commotion is all about.

But I've already fled the scene. I'm barreling down the hill in a blur of flannel penguins, my backpack flapping violently against my back, a new piece of evidence clutched tightly in my hand. I don't have time to examine it closely, but I already know what it is.

The Prowler has finally made a mistake.

And I have to warn Trex.

Trex

I splash cold water on my face, hoping the sudden chill will make the visions go away.

No such luck.

What began as an awesome virtual-reality edition of *Legends of Oren* has quickly turned into something else. Something I don't understand.

An image flashes inside my head. It's a family on the beach, sitting on a blanket. They're smiling, their hair tousled by the wind. The father is holding the little boy on his lap. The boy is reaching up to touch his father's cheek. The mother is gazing at them both, beaming. But I don't recognize them. Are they real? Or are they as fictional as the peasants in Oren? And why are they popping up in my brain?

I run a nubby washcloth over my face, which leaves me red and splotchy. I lean in and squint at my own reflection. It looks the same as always. It's only when I close my eyes again that things get confusing. This time, I see a zoomed-in picture of the little boy from the beach. My eyes instantly flutter open, and there's me again, twelve years old but looking suddenly much older. The contours of the little boy's face are still there.

The kid in the photograph is *me*.

I know that with a certainty I can't explain. But who are those other people? Why are they holding me? Why are they looking at me like that?

I've heard about repressed memories coming back to people years after a traumatic event, like a car accident. Maybe the strange headache I had earlier knocked something loose in my brain—hidden memories of long-forgotten relatives or something. Or maybe I'm just losing it.

The image changes again, as if someone has clicked to the next slide on a projector. The picture of the family is still there, but smaller, zoomed out this time. The photo is surrounded by columns of writing. It's the front page of a newspaper. Dated eight years ago. The date of my accident. Above it, a headline comes into focus: *Fatal Car Crash Claims Three Lives.*

But that doesn't make any sense . . .

"Have you seen my bow tie?" calls Mom, knocking on the bathroom door. I open my eyes, and the newspaper article disappears. "The hideous one from my uniform? I can't find it."

"No," I say, staring into my drawn face in the mirror but seeing only that little boy, laughing on the beach. "I haven't seen it."

"Oh well," she sighs. "Gary's going to dock my pay for that one. I'm heading to the café now. Are you okay?"

"Yeah," I say. "I'm . . . okay."

I listen to the sounds of Mom collecting her keys, walking through the front door, and starting the car's engine. Then I close my eyes and the article appears again. *Fatal Car Crash Claims Three Lives.* But only two people died that night. My father and the other driver. Who was the third person?

I feel sick. Dizzy. I lurch to the toilet and sink down beside it, my arms wrapped around the cool porcelain. But nothing comes up. My insides just churn angrily. I gulp deep breaths down my throat, forcing my eyes to stay open. Even the view of the rusting toilet is better than the images in my head. But I'm not strong enough to stop it. I blink, and another vision appears.

This time it's Mom—a much younger version, wearing a fancy suit and a serious expression. Her presence in my head is reassuring, even though I don't know what she's doing there or why she's dressed that way.

Then another headline appears, floating just above Mom's picture.

Accident Victim Kidnapped; Suspect on the Run.

Everything inside me comes gushing out at last, straight into the toilet.

CHAPTER 30

Brick

The first time Trex called me Mom, I opened my mouth to correct him. He'd woken from a bad dream and was babbling something about monsters. I swept into his room (which was really just a corner of the hotel room) and cradled his warm body, slick with sweat. I remember thinking that he felt just like a real boy, then shoving that thought out of my head. Of course he was real. What else would he be?

And then he mumbled, "Mom." He didn't know what he was saying, still in that hazy place between awake and asleep. I almost woke him up and set him straight, but I stopped myself. What was the harm in letting him say the word? What was the harm in both of us, perhaps, believing it? We were each alone in the world. Why not be each other's family?

I haven't forgotten for one instant that Trex already had a family when I met him—a real family. I know you can't just swap out someone's parents like actors in a TV show. But when we left the lab in the middle of the night, I never looked back. I never learned his biological parents' names or faces. I was afraid that if I did, they'd become real—to me and to him. Maybe Trex's dad really was a paleontologist. Maybe not. But that's the story I stuck with. All because of a T-shirt.

I didn't become a mother in the traditional way. I wasn't handed a wailing baby, slimy and red-faced. My child came to me on a metal gurney, unconscious and near death. He arrived as part of my job, a task I was told to carry out. Then taking care of him became my only job. The most important job I'd ever have. And one I clearly wasn't qualified for.

Who knew parenthood came with such worry, such consuming unease? Who knew it could cause an otherwise-rational person—a scientist!—to abandon all sense? I never intended to become a spy, for goodness' sake. I just wanted to make sure Trex made it to school that first morning without incident. And then there was Mellie. And Harrison. And an unprecedented drought. And lightning springing from Trex's fingertips. How could I let him face all of that alone? I'm the closest thing he has to a mother, after all. I've always planned to tell him everything, when he's ready, when the time is right. But the right time is a moving target—always next week, next month, next year. What if he resents me once he learns the truth? What if he sees me differently?

What if he stops calling me Mom?

CHAPTER 31

Mellie

"**Your mother is the** Prowler!" I gasp, holding up the sparkly red bow tie I found in Mr. Galleki's backyard. The same one she wears to work at the Plate of the Union Café.

Trex isn't quite looking at me, even though I'm standing right in front of him on his doorstep. His eyes are distant, like he's watching something I can't see.

"All this time, I'd assumed the Prowler was a man," I say breathlessly. "It was sexist of me and violated one of the most important rules of sleuthing: A good detective never makes assumptions. I'm planning to devote an entire chapter to this in my memoir. But I digress."

Still, Trex doesn't react. This is earth-shattering news, and he just stares at me like a zombie, which is frankly annoying. He hasn't even congratulated me on my exceptional detective-ing.

"My mother isn't here," he mumbles.

"Yeah, I know. I just saw her drive off. That's how I knew the coast was clear. I had to tell you—"

Trex pokes me, lightly, on the shoulder.

"What was that for?" I ask.

"I wanted to make sure you're real," he says.

"Umm, okay. Trex, you don't look so good." His skin is paler than usual, and he smells slightly acidic, like vomit.

"Something strange is happening," he says.

"Yeah, I know. Your mom is stalking you. When you said she was paranoid, I didn't think you meant stalker-level paranoid."

"That's not what I mean," he says.

"What's going on?" I ask.

"I hate her," he says.

"I'm sure she was just trying to protect you. She was worried about you. That's what moms do." I think of my own mom, standing uncomfortably in my room with a plastic cup, but I quickly push the thought aside. There are more pressing matters to worry about at the moment.

"She's not my mom," he says. His voice matches the look in his eyes—robotic and faraway. "My real mother died in the car accident. Mom just happened to be there, working in the lab where they patched me up. She kidnapped me."

"What?!" I blurt out. "That's crazy. What makes you think that?"

"They told me."

"Who told you?"

"The Company."

"I—I don't understand." I back away from him slightly, ready to bolt back home. The intensity on his face, the words coming out of his mouth . . . it's all sending shivers up my spine.

"Something has changed," he says. "In my head. I'm seeing things. Images and messages. The Company is trying to tell me something."

"Are you saying they . . . hacked you?"

"I don't know. Maybe. First, I got this horrible headache, and now I'm having these visions. I know things I shouldn't know. And I have no idea how I know them."

"Trex, that's awful," I say. "It's also kind of cool, though. In a bizarro, sci-fi-novel kind of way."

"It's mostly awful," says Trex.

"If The Company is really in your brain, they're probably feeding you lies," I say. "You've got no reason to trust them. About your mom or anything else."

"I don't know what to think," he says. "The things they're showing me look so real." He finally breaks out of his trance and looks at me. His eyes are desperate. I sigh with relief. Trex—the real Trex—is still in there.

"Come here," I say, pushing past him and sitting down at the computer in the living room. I nudge the mouse, and the screen flashes to life, displaying results from the most recent internet search. *Dry lightning strikes in Winnemucca, Nevada.* How strange. I start to read about dry lightning, but over my shoulder, I feel Trex practically vibrating. I pull up a new search. "Okay, tell me everything."

Trex describes newspaper articles about the car accident and the kidnapping. I type in keywords, and we both hold our breath as the results load on the screen. A photograph of Mrs. Wilson appears, next to an article labeling her a fugitive. It says she kidnapped a little boy from his room at the hospital. The boy was still recovering from his injuries after a major car accident, one in which he lost both his parents. *Both.*

"That's it," says Trex. His eyes have gone glassy again. "That's exactly what The Company showed me. They're not lying."

"I don't know what to say, Trex. I'm so sorry."

"I look nothing like her," he says. "And we don't have any photos from before the accident, except one blurry picture of my dad and me. She's not even in it. I always thought it was too painful for her to see old pictures of my dad. I thought it made her too sad. But it turns out she didn't even know him. She never even met him. I just . . . I feel like such an idiot."

"Why would she do it, though? Why steal a sick little boy?"

"Because the stuff in my head is worth a boatload," snarls Trex. "She's not even a waitress, you know. She's some super-smart scientist. Maybe she wanted The

Company's technology. Or maybe she's just some psycho who wanted a kid. Who knows?"

"I can't believe it."

"Yeah, that makes two of us," he says, through a clenched jaw. Over my shoulder, I can feel heat coming off him in waves. "She's been lying to me my entire life, Mellie. Every time we avoided the neighbors and moved to a new city, every time she refused to send me to school—it wasn't because she was afraid of The Company. She was afraid of getting caught. I've been living a lie so she could protect herself. She's a criminal. A . . . a liar."

He flexes his fingers. They're glowing eerily blue. I shrink away from him.

"And not only that," he says, his voice rising. "She kept me from my real family all this time. From ever knowing who they were. I hate her, Mellie, I really do."

A jagged beam of light shoots from his left hand to the computer. A wisp of smoke rises up from it, and the screen fades to black. Mrs. Wilson's image slowly disappears.

Trex

"You have to stop doing that!" says Mellie, pushing away from the fizzing computer.

"Sorry," I grumble.

"If you want to figure out what's going on, you can't electrocute everything in your path. Give me your phone. You can't be trusted with it." She holds out her palm, and I hand it over. I almost smile. Bossy, detective-mode Mellie is just what I need. "What's the real name of The Company?" she asks.

"I have no idea. Mom always calls it The Company. She never told me the real name."

"Well, that's not helpful. I guess I can try searching for companies that specialize in brain technology."

While Mellie taps away on the screen, I close my eyes and try to remember everything Mom has ever told me about The Company. The CEO had an unusual name. Kellen, maybe? Keller? No, Kellerman. As soon as I remember the name, I get a result.

"The Human Engineering Company," I blurt out.

"Excuse me?"

"That's The Company's real name."

"How do you know?" asks Mellie.

I give her a blank stare.

"Oh, right, you just *know*."

I wish I had a better explanation for what's happening to me, but I don't. The only thing I can compare it to is being in the darkest room I've ever seen, with blackout curtains and everything. Not a single sliver of light. There's endless nothing in every direction, but the nothing pulses like something's on the other side of it. Like *everything* is on the other side of it. All I have to do is focus, and whatever I'm thinking about materializes out of the nothing. It's sudden and surprising, like getting an idea. One instant it's not there—the next instant it is.

Mellie types the name into my phone. "Here it is . . . 'The Human Engineering Company operates at the intersection of medicine and technology, developing cutting-edge devices that save lives.'"

"That must be it."

"Oh, I get it!" says Mellie, her eyes lighting up. "The Human Engineering Company. T.H.E. Company."

"It's definitely them," I say.

"They have a list of offices on their website, but none of them are anywhere near Hopewell."

"1801 Baumgarten Boulevard," I say.

"You're really freaking me out with that," Mellie says as she types in the address.

"That makes two of us," I mumble, shaking my head to dislodge the printed words stamped across my vision.

Mellie frowns. "That's an industrial building about a mile from here. According to the records, it's unoccupied."

"The records are wrong," I say. "Let's go."

"Whoa, you can't be serious. I can name approximately a hundred reasons why that's a terrible idea. Number one: nothing good ever happens in an abandoned warehouse. It's a fact."

"We have to hurry, before Mom gets home."

"Trex, these people gave you a blinding headache. They hacked your brain. Now you're just going to do whatever they tell you to do?"

"They want to help me."

"Let me guess—did *they* tell you that?"

I nod.

"What if your mom—or whoever she is—is right? What if these people want to lure you to their building to lock you up and do experiments on you?"

"Between Mom and The Company, only one is a proven liar," I say.

"I've got a bad feeling about this," says Mellie. "Every good detective has a keen sense of intuition and—"

"I have to go," I say, moving toward the door. "The Company knows the truth about what happened eight years ago, and they understand what's going on in my head. They can give me answers. They can fix me."

"Who said you were broken?" asks Mellie, following me to the front door. "You're not a toaster, Trex."

"Are you coming with me or not?" I ask, striding outside. Barnaby plods along beside me, but I nudge him back into the house. He'll thank me when I can give him a proper scratch without charring his fur. But for now, he looks at me with sad pleading eyes as I leave.

"You of all people should know that every scary movie begins with some bonehead move like this," says Mellie, scurrying to keep up with me.

"I'm going," I say. "With or without you."

We reach the sidewalk. Mellie sighs and chews on her lip, debating her next move. On the one hand, she thinks I'm making a huge mistake. On the other hand, she can't resist a good mystery. And this one is a doozy.

"But my parents . . ." A dark look passes over her face, and for a moment, I think she'll choose to stay. Despite what I just said, the thought of going alone terrifies me. "And my pants!" Mellie groans, gesturing to her ridiculous penguin pajamas. "And it's getting late. Let's do this tomorrow. I'll come with you then, I promise."

But tomorrow will be too late. Mom will make sure I never make it to The Company if she finds out what I'm planning. Mellie is right—it's hazy and dark outside, almost night. But someone is at The Company, urging me to come to them. It's time.

"Are you in or out?" I say, waving off Mellie's concerns.

"Fine," she groans. "But if we make it through this alive, I'm looking for a new sidekick."

As I lead us down the hill, Mellie pores over The Company's website on my cell phone. "Wait a minute," she says. "Is *this* the evil scientist Mrs. Wilson is scared of?" She holds up the phone to show me a photo of a scrawny, middle-aged white man in a long lab coat that seems to swallow him up, like he borrowed it from his dad. He wears glasses with lenses the size of baseballs.

He sits at a large, expensive-looking desk, but he looks out-of-place and bewildered.

"Yep, that's Kellerman Vogel III, CEO of The Company," I say, matching the photo in Mellie's hand to the one I saw moments ago in my brain. "Mom says he's a genius. And ruthless."

"Hmph," says Mellie. "I guess looks can be deceiving. The first time I saw you, I thought you were completely unremarkable."

"I wish," I grumble under my breath. "We have to turn the phone off now."

"What?" Mellie gasps. "Why? It's our only connection to the outside world."

"Exactly. Which means Mom can track it. If I leave it on, she'll follow me."

"I guess we don't really need it," says Mellie, reluctantly powering my phone down, "since we've got your super-brain."

"It's not the same thing. My brain isn't a computer."

"Oh yeah? Then where are we going?" Without even realizing it, I've veered off the main road in the direction of The Company's building. Somehow I know the way. "See." She grins at me. "It's so cool. You'll never need a data plan again. What's 167 times 83?"

"No way." I shake my head. "I'm not here for your entertainment."

"C'mon," says Mellie, nudging me with her elbow. "You know you want to."

She's right. I *am* a little curious about my newfound abilities. I focus on the question: 167 x 83. But I get nothing in response.

"I don't know the answer," I say. "It's like . . . I can access certain things but not others."

"Ah, I get it," says Mellie, nodding like all of this makes perfect sense. "The Company will only let you see what they want you to see. Kind of like they turned on parental controls inside your head."

"Yeah, I guess," I say. "But as soon as we reach The Company, I'm going to ask them to shut it down."

"You mean, you'll ask them to turn off the parental controls, right? So you can fully harness your powers?"

"Nope." I firmly shake my head. "I want them to shut it all down. I don't need a supercomputer brain."

"What?!" gasps Mellie. "You've got to be kidding! That's like Sherlock Holmes giving up his powers of deduction." Mellie gazes up at me with wide eyes. Her curtain of hair is swept to the side, showing her entire face for once, and it looks thoroughly stunned.

"His powers of *what*?"

"Ugh. It's like . . . like Spider-Man having his . . . web fingers removed."

"Web fingers?" I chuckle. "I really need to introduce you to a Marvel movie. Besides, I already told you, I'm not a superhero."

"I disagree," says Mellie. "You used your lightning powers to fight the villain known as Harrison Palmer."

"Yeah, and we saw how well that worked out."

"But your brain makes you . . . you. You can't give that up."

"I just want to be normal," I say. "Don't you?"

"Sometimes," she says, shrugging. "But I've got this theory that feeling like a weirdo in middle school *is* normal. I think Harrison and Ridley are the real freaks here."

I consider this for a moment, then shake my head. All my life, I've wanted an ordinary, standard-issue brain. And this is my chance to get one.

I pick up the pace in the direction of The Company.

CHAPTER 32

Mellie

Trex and I trudge the streets of Hopewell. We pass from the busy center of town into the quiet neighborhoods beyond and finally find ourselves surrounded by large, empty stretches of land covered in scorched patches of dead grass. I haven't seen another person in a half hour. Not even a cow. It's not exactly inspiring confidence in this whole operation.

"I still remember my first stomachache," I say, out of the blue.

I'm not sure why I'm bringing this up now. Maybe because adrenaline is coursing through my body, and I want someone to know my story before I embark upon the most dangerous, most exciting thing I've ever done. Or maybe because Trex needs to hear it.

"Really?" he asks.

"I was seven years old," I say. "It happened at Ridley's birthday party. Believe it or not, Ridley and I used to be friends. Danica, too. Ridley invited us both to her party. I thought it was just going to be a few kids from the neighborhood having pizza and cake, but when I got there, I couldn't believe my eyes. Her parents had decked the place out. She had a bounce house, face painting, even a pony. And she'd invited practically the entire school. It was great. Until it wasn't. After a little while, I started to feel . . . not right."

"A stomachache?"

"No, not exactly. At least not at first. I just felt a little tired. I found Mother talking to the other moms in the kitchen and told her I wanted to go home. She waved me off and told me to go play. Then I found Father watching baseball with the dads, and he told me the same thing. *Go play with the other kids.* But I didn't want to go play with the other kids. So I snuck down the hall to Ridley's room and started playing with her dolls."

"And then you got sick?"

"Actually, I was starting to feel better when Mrs. Duncan found me. She told me it was time for cake. I told her I wanted to stay where I was, but she said Ridley wanted me to be there when she blew out the candles. I told her I didn't feel well, that I needed to lie down. I felt . . . drained."

"I know the feeling," says Trex.

I squirm, dreading the next part of the story. The worst

part. "Mrs. Duncan said I wasn't allowed to be in the bedrooms by myself, that I had to join the party. By then, I *did* have a stomachache. A bad one. But I did what I was told. Mrs. Duncan gave me a seat right next to the birthday girl. The candles were lit, and everyone started to sing. Ridley was just about to blow out the candles when I started to feel woozy. And then . . . well . . . all that pizza I'd had for lunch came bubbling back up. . . ."

"No!" gasped Trex.

"Yes. I puked all over Ridley's birthday cake. Her fancy party was like a war zone after that—people screaming in panic and running in all directions. Ridley crying her eyes out. Mrs. Duncan wailing. I ran out the front door, all the way back home. All the way to my room. And that was the last time I hung out with those kids. With any kids, really."

Telling the story brings me right back to that party. I'll never forget the expression on my parents' faces as they made apologies for me and scrambled to clean up my mess. They looked mortified. Why couldn't their daughter just play in the bounce house like all the other kids?

"Wow," says Trex. "That sounds awful."

"It was. It really was."

We fall silent, but then a sudden snort escapes from the back of Trex's throat. "I'm sorry," he says, in the strained voice of someone trying to hold in a laugh. "It's not funny."

"You're right," I say, glaring at him. "It isn't. It was traumatic! When vomit exploded all over Ridley's perfect pink cake and splashed on her perfect pink princess dress, it was . . . it was . . ." I erupt in laughter, forgetting for a brief moment my own humiliation and remembering the furious, horrified look on Ridley's face. ". . . hilarious."

"The Princess of Puke!" he says. "It suits her, I think."

"The Baroness of Barf!" I add.

"The Duke of Hurl!" says Trex, laughing so hard he has to stop and catch his breath. "This game might be the new Alphabetter!"

I'm racking my brain for another synonym for "puke," my cheeks sore from smiling, when Trex's laughter suddenly fades.

"Um . . . Mellie?" he says. His expression darkens as he gazes at something in the distance, over my shoulder.

"What's wrong?" I ask, turning around. Then I stop laughing, too.

"We're here."

Trex

Mom doesn't let me watch scary movies, but I know Mellie is right—they all start just like this. With a couple of dumb kids rushing headfirst into danger. If I were watching myself on a screen right now, I'd have my hands over my eyes, peering through the space between my fingers, shouting "Stop! Don't do it! You're an idiot!"

While we were busy laughing about vomit-covered birthday cake, we ventured far away from the main road, beyond Hopewell's shops and schools and houses, to a dull gray industrial park at the edge of town. 1801 Baumgarten Boulevard is a flat, boring building in a row of flat, boring buildings, with a giant parking lot in front and a creepy wooded area in back. In the scary movie, I'm pretty sure that's where the bodies are buried. There are no cars in the parking lot. No indication that anyone is here at all. The building's few windows are boarded up with plywood.

"Are you sure this is the right address?" asks Mellie.

"Positive," I say. And I am.

"You know, Pancake Hut is open twenty-four hours," she says hopefully.

"They're in there," I say, trying to sound more confident than I feel. "I'm going in." I march to the front door, which is made of reinforced steel, like at a maximum-security prison. I press the buzzer with the bony part of my elbow, to avoid a shock. Mellie scurries after me.

"Did you know the human brain produces enough electricity to power a light bulb?" she says. "That's for an average brain. Yours could probably power one of those giant spotlights they use to call Batman. I was re- searching brains last night. When I couldn't sleep."

Nobody answers the door, so I jab the buzzer again. And again. After each buzz, I pause to listen for foot- steps. Every time, I hear only silence.

"Maybe they want you to come back in the morning, when they're ready for visitors," says Mellie. "They're clearly just moving in. They need to tidy up. Mother hates when people show up unannounced. She always pretends she's not home."

"It's not unannounced," I say. "They brought me here."

"Did you know the Pancake Hut has twenty-seven flavors of pancakes? I don't know how many different syrups they have, but it's a lot. I bet your super-brain could calculate all the different pancake-and-syrup com- binations. Want to try it?"

I look at Mellie with lifted eyebrows, an expression I learned from Mom. A what-the-heck-are-you-talking- about? expression.

"Sorry," she says. "It appears I blabber when I'm in mortal danger. I've never been in mortal danger before, so I never knew this detail about myself. It's surprising because I'm usually so quiet, but—"

A latch clicks, and Mellie groans. I try the door handle—zapping it in the process—and it turns. I pull the door open with painful slowness. It's as heavy as it looks. Something gurgles behind me.

"Sorry," whispers Mellie, clutching her stomach. I can't say that I blame her for having butterflies. I step inside, and she follows. As soon as she's over the threshold, the door swings shut behind us with a tremendous thud. The lock clicks back into place.

The building is even creepier on the inside. Fluorescent lights flicker and hiss above us, some of them hanging out of their sockets. Plaster is peeling off the walls. I can see right down to the steel beams in some places. Worst of all, there's not a soul in sight. We walk slowly down a long, deserted hallway. The rooms on either side of us are empty, except for a few stray desks, boxes, and office chairs.

"Nobody's here," Mellie whispers. "We should go."

Then a man steps out of the shadows.

"Trex?" he says, peering down the hallway at me. It's the man from the website—the same oversized lab coat, the same comically big glasses. He pushes them up the bridge of his nose with one finger. He squints at us for a moment; then his face breaks into a smile. "Welcome to The Company. We've been waiting for you."

CHAPTER 33

Mellie

There's no changing Trex's mind. Not with The Company literally *inside* it. If I were reading this in a book right now, I'd slam it shut and drop it off at the Little Free Library—or else I'd chuck it against a wall for having such boneheaded main characters.

"I'm Dr. Kellerman Vogel," says the man rushing toward us. He approaches Trex as if he's greeting a celebrity, only he doesn't quite know what to do with his hands. First he goes for a handshake; then he thinks better of it and leans in for a half hug. He finally winds up patting Trex on the shoulder. It's so awkward. How this guy runs a multimillion-dollar company is beyond me. I take back what I said about respecting anyone who dresses like a real doctor. "I see you received our messages."

"Yes," says Trex, and I notice him shudder. He must

be remembering the headache. Or the traumatic visions that followed.

"I don't typically approve of such invasive tactics," says Vogel, "but my hands were tied. We tried contacting you numerous times, but our attempts were always thwarted by your, er, caretaker. The only way we could reach you was by direct intervention, which could only be accomplished once we knew your precise location. I apologize for the unpleasantness, but you're here now, and that's what matters. Who's your friend?" He slides his eyes to me, lingering on my penguin pants.

"This is Mellie," says Trex. "She knows about my brain and . . . everything."

"Oh," says Vogel, a worried look passing over his face. "Is that so? Well, what's done is done. In the future, though, we insist on strict confidentiality here at The Company. For your own protection, of course."

"Of course," says Trex. "Sorry."

"Don't fret," says Vogel. "Let's just make sure it doesn't happen again, all right?"

Trex nods. Vogel gives me a tight-lipped smile. And I see it, a brief but unmistakable flash of ice in his eyes—cold and hard. My intuition starts leaping up and down, waving a bright red flag.

"I know you've come here for answers," Vogel continues, addressing Trex. "And more than that, you've been experiencing some changes lately. You need our help."

"Yes," says Trex, his head bobbing up and down in a vigorous nod.

"I can provide you with both. I saved your life once, and I can do it again. But first"—he claps his hands together—"let's get a few precautions out of the way. Lou!"

Another figure appears at the far end of the hallway. At first, I can't tell if it's a man or a large, lumbering beast. Whatever Lou is, he fills the hallway from top to bottom and left to right, and he's coming straight at us.

"Yeah, boss?" says Lou. Apparently it's a man. An impossibly massive one.

"Can you please perform a security check on our guests?" says Vogel.

Lou grunts in reply. He steps up to me, his oversized muscles straining the seams of his T-shirt. He wears a fierce but slightly confused expression, like he's angry but not sure why. He nods at my backpack. I scowl, but I'm not going to argue with a mutant man-beast. I hand it over.

"It's purely precautionary," explains Vogel, while Lou riffles through my stuff. "As you can imagine, we do very sophisticated and sensitive work here. Our competitors would love to get their hands on our research. As would some of our, er, detractors. We must be very careful."

Lou removes Trex's phone from my backpack and hands it to Vogel. Then he whispers in Vogel's ear, and the doctor nods. "I'm afraid we must hold on to this while you are on the premises," says Vogel. "It will be returned to you when you leave. If that's acceptable, you may follow me."

Trex and I lock eyes.

Mine say: *Let's go to the Pancake Hut.*

Trex's say: *I'm a zombie controlled by The Company, so I'm staying.*

What choice do I have? A good detective doesn't leave her sidekick alone with a man-beast and an evil scientist disguised as a nerd. Even if her sidekick *is* a gullible half-wit.

Vogel walks briskly ahead of us down another hallway, and we scurry after him. "Please excuse our mess," he says over his shoulder. "We acquired this space just last week and are still getting settled." The offices in this wing of the building contain sleek metal furniture and stacks of unopened boxes. The desks are cluttered with computer monitors, loose cables, and mountains of paper. Only one room we pass seems to be completely furnished—a surgical suite, complete with a padded table, blinking machines, and trays full of gleaming instruments. Another man in a lab coat stands with his back to us, fiddling with dials. Trex and I slow down to peer inside, and I send another message with my eyes: *This is where they'll dismantle you for parts, you dingdong.* Trex's eyes say: *Cool. Shiny!* I definitely need a new sidekick. Dr. Vogel hurries us along with an "ahem."

"What sort of work will you do here?" asks Trex, practically jogging to keep pace with Vogel's long strides.

"Put simply, we'll maximize human potential," says Vogel, and I roll my eyes. Luckily, nobody's paying any attention to me. "I began my career in neurology, but my research on the brain sparked a growing interest in robotics and electronics. More specifically, I wanted to explore how the two fields intersect. I knew that was the future. So I brought together the foremost experts in medicine and technology, and collectively, we build the things that help humans live better, longer, and more productive lives."

"Like my brain?" asks Trex, his voice too eager.

"Precisely," says Vogel. "Despite what you may have been told, we are trying to save the world, one breakthrough at a time. Starting, of course, with you."

This time, I can't help it. A derisive snort bursts from the back of my throat. Vogel turns around and glares at me, and I spot it again. The *real* Kellerman Vogel III. But when Trex looks over, Vogel plasters a wide smile on his face. Trex, totally duped, smiles back.

Trex

I relax. Dr. Vogel is nothing like Mom said. Just more evidence that she's a big fat liar. Dr. Vogel guides us into his office, which is out of place in this spooky old building. It's fully decorated, with a big polished desk, squishy chairs, and paintings on the walls that look expensive. Dr. Vogel settles into his chair and swivels around a few times before he speaks. "Let's get down to business. Would you like to hear the story of what happened to you after your accident? The *real* story?"

"Yes," I say. "Please."

"Good. You should never shy away from the truth, no matter how, er, unpleasant it may be. On the night of the accident, you and your mother arrived at our hospital in critical condition. Your father died at the scene. This much you know."

I nod.

"Everything else you've been told is a lie."

I suck in my breath. I knew this was coming, but it still knocks the wind out of me. I brace myself for what's next.

"Your mother died in the ER shortly after she arrived. You were declared brain-dead. In any other hospital, you would've died, too, just like your parents. But you had the good fortune to arrive at my doorstep. The doctors rushed you into surgery, but it wasn't a standard procedure. I was there, along with top medical engineers from The Company. Together, we replaced over forty percent of your damaged brain tissue with our proprietary technology. We operated on you for over seven hours. During that time, you flatlined twice. And twice, we brought you back."

I gasp. Mom never told the story this way. She never mentioned a seven-hour surgery or the two times my heart stopped. She certainly never mentioned Kellerman Vogel having been in the operating room.

"I'm not going to sugarcoat it, Trex. This technology had never worked before. All our other subjects died. But you lived. We monitored your progress twenty-four hours a day after that, afraid you'd crash at any moment. But you fared better than anyone expected. Your condition went from critical to stable in forty-eight hours. We saved your life." Dr. Vogel is no longer unsure of himself. It's like he's in his element now, talking about my surgery. He leans forward and holds my gaze.

"W-was *she* there?" I ask, still not sure what to call the-woman-formerly-known-as-Mom.

"I assume you mean Brick," says Dr. Vogel. "No, Brick wasn't in the operating room. She was a brilliant scientist, but she was no surgeon."

"Brick?"

"Yes, the woman who took you. That was her nickname—Britt the Brick. We called her that because she was my most trusted employee. I guess the joke was on me."

Britt the Brick? Mom, a waitress working double shifts at a crummy diner to make ends meet, was once a neuroscientist known as Britt the Brick? Have I been sucked into an alternate universe? At this point, Miles Morales could burst into the room, and it wouldn't even faze me.

"Brick was responsible for monitoring you once you came out of the OR," Vogel says. "She had the graveyard shift. She volunteered for it, in fact. One night when she was alone in the lab, out of the blue, she took you off the machines that were helping you stay alive, and she disappeared."

"But why?" I ask. "Why would she do that?" Anger bubbles up in me like hot liquid. I feel it coursing through my veins, rushing toward my fingertips.

"I can't pretend to understand her reasoning," says Dr. Vogel. "All I know is she put you at serious risk then, and you've been in danger ever since. What if something had gone wrong with your implant? She may be a gifted scientist, but without The Company's resources, she would have no way of saving you."

My chest begins to heave as these words sink in. She risked my life for her own selfish whim. And this man did the opposite. A sharp, crackling sound cuts through the air and zigzags of light pass between my fingers.

A twitchy smile plays on Dr. Vogel's lips when he notices my surge of electricity. "I'm relieved you came to us," he says. "You're at a critical juncture, Trex. Your own body will destroy you if we don't fix it soon."

I ball my hands into fists and shove them under my thighs.

"Don't be embarrassed," he says. "That charge means the product is working. The electricity is moving to your fingertips instead of your brain. But my team can make it less uncomfortable for you with just a simple download."

"Really? You can make me . . . normal?" I ask, my

heart fluttering at the thought. I glance over at Mellie, expecting her to be happy for me, but she's staring at Dr. Vogel with squinty eyes. Leave it to Mellie to be skeptical of the one person who can help me.

"Is that what you want?" asks Dr. Vogel. "To be normal?"

"Yes. More than anything."

Dr. Vogel sinks back into his chair and frowns. "I have to admit, Trex, I'm a little disappointed."

"Huh?"

"It's just that I expected more from you. After everything you've overcome to get here, I'm surprised you'd settle for ordinary."

"But—"

"You're not like the rest of us, Trex. You're already a medical marvel, and you have the capacity to be even greater. We've had years to develop upgrades to your technology, functionality unlike anything you've ever dreamed of." His eyes glitter behind the big glasses. "Let me make you extraordinary."

Mellie

Trex falters, finally. Vogel's baloney about making him "extraordinary" isn't working. Hopefully Trex sees now what a fraud this guy is. Surely my healthy skepticism has worn off on him.

"How rude of me," says Vogel, abruptly changing the subject. "You two must be famished, and I haven't offered you any refreshments. We haven't got much, but I'm sure we can scrounge something up for our guests." He removes a small yellow walkie-talkie from a clip on his belt and barks into it, "Lou! Refreshments!"

Moments later—way too soon for "scrounging"— Lou appears, balancing a silver platter on his meaty hands. It contains two cans of soda and a plate of cookies. Familiar pale cookies dusted with cinnamon-sugar.

Snickerdoodles.

Pain suddenly grips my midsection.

"Mellie," says Vogel, "have a drink. Ginger ale, perhaps?" He motions to the can nearest me on the tray and winks. My heart momentarily stops. Holding my breath, I reach out and wrap my fingers around it. It's room temperature. Room-temperature ginger ale.

How'd they know my favorite drink?

How'd they know I'd even be here?

The pain in my stomach makes me hunch over in my seat.

We've been trailing Trex's mom around the neighborhood in her ridiculous costume while real, professional bad guys were prying into our lives and manipulating us. Even the kindly old man with the paper map was a spy. I can't believe I missed it. I can't believe they got one over on me. A good detective would've known. . . .

"You've probably realized by now that my associate has been doing some, er, let's call them reconnaissance missions in your neighborhood," says Vogel. "I sent Mack to Hopewell Hill to confirm that Trex was the right child—the one we'd lost track of. We had to find you, Trex, by any means necessary. Without intervention from The Company, your brain is likely to fail, or else your electrical charge will continue to increase and eventually kill you in any number of ways."

Another spasm of pain rips through me. What if I'm wrong about The Company? What if their motives really are benevolent? What if Trex really does need them to survive? What if I've been wrong about *everything*?

Worst of all, what if I'm . . . a *mediocre* detective? I bite my lip as the ache in my stomach radiates through my body. I start to shake. I look up at Vogel through a veil of hair and see a satisfied grin on his face.

I may have solved my puny little cases, but I missed the real mystery that was right under my nose. My big break, and I blew it. I'm no Sherlock Holmes or Myrtle Hardcastle. I'm barely even a Watson. I'm useless.

I hate to give Vogel the satisfaction, but I can't help it. I reach for that can of ginger ale. I crack it open and take a warm, soothing swig.

Trex

"I want to show you something," says Dr. Vogel. "A preview of what you can be." He grins, which somehow looks more like a grimace on him. He clicks the keys on his sleek, razor-thin computer, then hits Enter with a flourish. And then . . . nothing happens.

"Um . . ." My eyes dart around the room. "What am I waiting for?"

"You'll see," says Vogel. "When I accessed your brain earlier this afternoon, I gave you specific pieces of information, just enough to lead you here. But I've just removed all barriers, Trex. Now you can go anywhere, virtually speaking. It's best to start small so you don't get overwhelmed. Like . . . which film won the Academy Award for best original score in 1983?"

As soon as the question reaches my ears, I know the answer. I blurt out, "*E.T.*" Then I turn to Mellie. "167 times 83 is 13,861."

"Amazing, isn't it?" says Dr. Vogel. "All human knowledge is at your disposal, without the need for a phone or any other device. From now on, you'll be the smartest person in the room. In *any* room. We've beta tested similar technology in a headpiece—not nearly as seamless as your implant—and I must warn you, it can be rather disorienting. Some subjects lose touch with reality, become addicted, even after a brief period of time. Such abilities are not to be trifled with."

"I understand," I say, even though I don't. I feel the same as I did a minute ago. I don't feel like someone with a not-to-be-trifled-with ability. I glance over at Mellie, but she's chugging ginger ale, not even paying attention. Some detective.

"And networking is only the beginning," says Dr. Vogel.

"It is?"

"I gave you a preview of our virtual-reality product earlier, when you stepped into *Legends of Oren.* Do you want to visit Paris? Tokyo? The inside of a volcano? You can travel to all of those places without leaving your sofa. I'll give you another example." Vogel types another command into his computer.

Suddenly, I'm in the garden on Hopewell Hill. Vogel's office was stuffy and cramped, but here the sky feels wide open. The wind blows, and I can see each strand of hair on my arm flutter. The sun beats down on the Unnamed Girl, making her glow. I walk toward her, and she looks down at me like always, though her eyes are more distressed than usual. I reach out and touch her boot, like I did the night I made fireworks. The night I got mixed up with Mellie Chandler and didn't even know it. Only this time, no fireworks. Not even a spark. I run my fingers over the smooth, cool bronze. I'm touching metal. *I* am touching metal.

In the distance, I hear a clicking of keyboard keys, and the Unnamed Girl disappears. My hand is outstretched, stroking the surface of Dr. Vogel's shiny desk. I'm grinning like a fool. I drop both my hand and the grin and say, "Neat." With a shrug, like it's no big deal.

"Neat indeed," says Vogel. "And it's not just a collection of parlor tricks, either. I remember what it's like to be in middle school—the awkwardness, the angst." I try to imagine Dr. Vogel in sixth grade. There's no way that guy made it through middle school without a *lot* of teasing. "With the newest software update, we can supply you with the perfect script for any social situation. Anecdotes, comebacks, quips, slang. Our bots can scan thousands of popular websites to make sure you always have the perfect thing to say. You'll never be tongue-tied again!"

"That sounds awesome," I say. "But—"

"But *what*?" he says, with an almost-wounded look on his face.

How do I tell him that—despite everything he has to offer—I still want to be normal? That being an awkward, tongue-tied kid in middle school *is* normal, just like Mellie said?

"What could be more important than maximizing your potential?" he asks.

"Pee," Mellie blurts out suddenly. "I have to pee."

Mellie

Vogel sits in front of a boarded-up window, and the darkened glass behind him reflects the back of his head—a swirl of thin hair surrounding a prominent bald spot. It's not a pleasant sight, but it's less upsetting than what he's doing to Trex, so I let my eyes rest there. The ginger ale is doing its job, easing the rumbling in my stomach. But it also fills my bladder until I'm ready to burst.

"I have to pee," I blurt out.

Vogel rolls his eyes, but Trex seems grateful for the interruption. "Lou!" Vogel shouts into the walkie-talkie. When the beast appears in the doorway, Vogel orders him to escort me to the restroom. I rise from my seat, and a wave of dizziness sets my head spinning.

"Are you all right?" asks Trex, gazing at me with concern.

I steady myself against the back of the chair. I check in with my stomach, which is finally behaving itself. "I'm fine," I say.

I follow Lou's hulking back down a series of hallways to a small, dirty bathroom. I shut myself inside and take a deep breath. Maybe I can stay here. Maybe they'll forget about me.

Thoughts are whizzing nonstop around my brain, and I'm woozy trying to corral them. Or maybe I'm just plain woozy. I turn on the water and splash it on my face.

I catch a glimpse of myself in the chipped mirror, and my heart skids to a stop. Something is wrong with my reflected self. She's blurry. Her skin is rippling. I blink hard to bring her into focus, but she skims the glass like a stone skimming over the surface of the water.

I stumble out the door, tripping into Lou. He steadies me, but I break away from him. Somehow I remember the way back to Vogel's office. How do I know the way? I burst through the door like a banshee, startling Trex and Vogel. They look up in alarm as I stand there, swaying in the doorway like a stalk of wheat.

"Mellie?" says Trex. "Are you sure you're okay?"

I scan the room. My eyes dart from diplomas to books to paperweights.

None of those things are the thing I'm looking for.

Trex holds an open can of root beer—a cold one. He raises it to his lips.

That's it!

With ninja-like reflexes, I slap it out of his hand before he can take another sip. Soda sprays in a wide arc across the room, splashing Vogel's perfectly white lab coat. The can crashes to the ground.

Vogel roars. Trex gapes at me.

"Don't drink that!" I shout. "We've been drugged!"

CHAPTER 34

Trex

"That's complete nonsense!" huffs Dr. Vogel, dabbing at his lapel with a handkerchief. "Why would I drug a couple of kids?"

"Good question," snaps Mellie. Then, in an imitation of his stilted voice, she adds, "I can't pretend to understand your reasoning." I'm shocked by what she's saying, but even more shocked by this version of Mellie. She glares at Dr. Vogel as she mocks him. She's fearless. Possibly out of her mind, but still fearless.

Dr. Vogel smiles. "My dear, those cans of soda were closed when we gave them to you. How do you suppose we got drugs inside?"

Mellie wavers. I can't tell if she's thrown off by his question or just having a dizzy spell. I jump out of my chair and lower her into it. "She's definitely not okay," I say to Dr. Vogel. "Something isn't right."

Dr. Vogel sighs and shakes his head. "Do you want to tell him?" he asks Mellie.

"I already told him!" she cries, pointing a shaking finger at him. "*You* did this to me!"

"It's not my place to disclose this type of information," says Dr. Vogel, "but I'm afraid you have forced my hand, Melissa. I can't have Trex thinking of me as some monster who harms children."

"What's going on?" I ask, my eyes darting back and forth between them. "What's he talking about?"

Dr. Vogel sighs and hesitates before speaking. "When Lou checked your bags earlier, he found something in Mellie's backpack. A bottle of pills. Prescription medication."

"He's a liar!" Mellie shouts. "You can search my backpack. I've got nothing in there." She lifts her bag and unzips it. An orange pill bottle clatters to the floor. We both stare dumbstruck at it, then at each other.

"They planted that," she says.

I pick it up. It's identical to the one I found in her room, with Mellie's name and address printed on the label. Along with a string of words I don't understand. "She takes pills for stomachaches," I say. "So what?"

"Those are benzodiazepines," says Vogel. "They're used to treat psychiatric illnesses. They're not for stomachaches."

"Oh," I say, placing the bottle on the desk, still utterly confused. "I still don't see what the big deal is."

"The big deal, Trex, is that she's been dishonest. I can't say for sure what's causing . . . this." He waves his hand in Mellie's general direction, like she's a spill on the floor. "But I can assure you it has nothing to do with drugs in a can of ginger ale. I'm a doctor, Trex, so I mean no judgment, but Mellie has some issues she needs to address that have nothing to do with me."

"It's not true," whimpers Mellie, crumpling into her seat like a wilting flower.

"Don't worry," Dr. Vogel says to me. "If your friend needs medical attention, she's in the right place. I'll have my associates look after her while we begin your examination."

"My . . . what?"

"Your physical exam. We haven't checked your brain in eight years, and I shudder to think of the shape it's in now. We're just going to run some routine tests to see what's going on in there."

"I—I didn't realize you were going to start today," I say.

"There's no time to waste," says Vogel.

"No!" shrieks Mellie. "Trex, don't go! I don't trust them. Every good detective follows their insteps."

"Their . . . what?" I ask. Dr. Vogel shoots me an I-told-you-so look.

"Their in . . . ins . . . ," stutters Mellie.

I turn to Dr. Vogel. "You'll make sure she's okay?"

"Absolutely."

I hesitate. I don't want to leave Mellie in this state,

but I have to know what's going on in my head. Besides, Dr. Vogel said he'd take care of her. Just like he's helping me. I can trust him.

"All right," I say. "Let's do this."

Mellie

Trex leaves, and a familiar old man strides into the room. He looks completely different than he did when he approached us in the garden, asking for directions to Colorado Street. He's not stooped or shuffling in the slightest. In fact, when he stands up straight, his ropy muscles bulge against his polo shirt. "Howdy, neighbor," he says, smiling that same friendly, old-man smile. "You remember me, don't you? Mack?"

I scowl at him.

"I'm actually Dr. Stewart Mackenzie, head of software engineering at The Human Engineering Company, but you can still call me Mack." He settles into Vogel's plush chair and casually swings his legs onto the surface of the desk. Behind me, Lou stations himself at the door like a guard dog.

"I see you've met Lou," says Mack. "Don't be fooled by his appearance, though. He's a big teddy bear once you get to know him." I glance over my shoulder, and

Lou growls at me, more like a real-life bear than the stuffed kind.

"You tricked us!" I say to Mack. "And to think I helped you."

"Sorry, kid, but we had to make sure your little friend was the zapper. The fake names you gave me threw me off . . . for about ten seconds. As soon as I found the chatty little snot with the red cheeks, I had all the information I needed. Amazing how some baked goods can get people talking. After that, all I had to do was get within range of Trex's brain, work my magic, and . . . boom! I was in."

"Harrison," I hiss under my breath.

"Don't get too upset with the snitch," says Mack. "The Company would've found Trex one way or another."

"When? In another eight years?"

"Aren't you plucky?" chuckles Mack. "We'll see how long that lasts."

"What did you do to me?" I snarl.

"Now, don't be like that. You should be flattered, really. We've been watching you for a while, Melissa Chandler, and we knew you wouldn't go along with all this willingly. The boss wouldn't go to all this trouble to take you out of commission if he didn't think you were a serious threat. You should be honored."

"What are you talking about?"

"Haven't you figured it out yet? Hm, maybe you're not as smart as we thought."

He walks calmly around the desk and picks up the prescription bottle Trex left there. The one that allegedly belongs to me.

"Where did you get that?" Did they steal it from my house? Take out a prescription in my name? Create a fake label? Either way, the message is chillingly clear: The Company knows everything. And can get whatever it wants.

"According to our records, you have an active prescription for the treatment of generalized anxiety disorder and panic disorder. Is that right?" asks Mack.

"That's confidential!" I cry.

"How adorable," Mack says over my head to Lou. "She thinks personal information can still be 'confidential' in this day and age."

"I wanna see Trex," I say. "I wanna go home."

"Of course we'll let you go," says Mack. "As soon as the boss gives the word . . ."

"You won't get away with this! Let me go!" I leap from my seat and take a wobbly step forward, even though the floor is rippling and trying to buck me like a wild horse.

Lou is suddenly right behind me. His massive hands land heavily on my shoulders, pressing me back into the chair. "We can do this the easy way," he says, "or we can do this the hard way."

It's the cheesiest line I've ever heard someone say in real life, and even though I'm being kidnapped, held in place by a man who could crush me like a squirming bug, I guffaw. I start laughing and can't stop. The whole situation is terrifying, not remotely funny, but I keep on cackling. Lou backs away from me, my crazed laughter weirding him out.

"They're not paying me enough for this," grumbles Mack. "How much of that tranquilizer did you give her anyway?"

"Exactly what the boss said," says Lou. "Five milligrams."

"You mean *point* five milligrams," says Mack, his face draining of color. "Right?" He picks up my can of ginger ale and shakes it. The remaining liquid sloshes around at the bottom.

Lou's dimpled chin begins to quiver. "I think we've got a problem."

Trex

When I climb onto the padded table, it dawns on me that this is exactly what Mom feared. I'm about to be poked and prodded like a lab rat. High-voltage lamps shine down on me. Machines hum and beep. Everything around me is cold, sterile, and unwelcoming.

But this is how they'll fix me.

Dr. Vogel stands in a corner of the room, observing me with an unreadable expression on his face. Another white-coated man—the one I caught a glimpse of earlier—bustles around the room turning knobs with his head bowed.

"What are you going to do, exactly?" I ask.

"We'll start with a quick scan," says Dr. Vogel. "A completely routine procedure. Dr. Grayson here is one of the best neurosurgeons in the country. *The* best, if you ask me. You're in excellent hands."

Dr. Grayson approaches with a metal helmet that looks like an overturned colander. I remove my lucky baseball cap and clutch it tightly while the doctor straps the device onto my head. It's a bit too tight but otherwise seems harmless enough. Without a word, Dr. Grayson slinks back to his machines, with far less confidence than his boss.

"Since The Company deactivated your pain receptors, you won't feel a thing," Dr. Vogel adds. "A lifetime without physical pain—how's that for a side effect?"

"Pretty great," I admit. "Until this afternoon."

"Ah, yes. Activation of the technology's full suite of features can be jarring."

"And there was this one time, when I was eight, when I got a second-degree burn on my arm because I didn't realize I was leaning on a hibachi grill. That was pretty jarring, too."

"You make an excellent point," says Dr. Vogel, stroking his chin. "Sometimes pain has its benefits. Your accident, for example. It was a tragic event by all accounts, but look what it led to. What we learn by studying your technology will save thousands of lives."

"Really?"

"Absolutely. The only reason we haven't made huge advancements already is because of *her*."

He says "her" with disgust, and I know he means Mom.

"If we'd had access to your brain for the last eight years, we could have made significant improvements by now. We could have helped countless numbers of people. We will never know how many others like you have died in emergency rooms since your accident."

His words make the blood run cold in my veins. I've been so consumed with my own story, it hasn't occurred to me that other people may have been affected by what Mom did. That other people may have died because of it.

"What's going to happen to her?" I ask. "To . . . Brick?"

"I don't know," says Dr. Vogel. "Jail, most likely. Probably for the rest of her life."

I gasp. I imagine the Mom I know—paranoid, overprotective, gentle—sitting in a jail cell. She'll never survive.

"I know you care for her, Trex, and I'm sure she's done a fine job raising you up to this point, but we can't allow people to go around kidnapping orphaned children just because they feel like it."

"I—I know what she did was wrong," I say, "but you don't really think she deserves to go to jail, do you? Now that you have me back, can't you just let her go?"

Dr. Vogel shrugs. "It's not for me to say, Trex. Or you, either. That's for the authorities to decide. Remember, she didn't just take a child. She took millions of dollars' worth of intellectual property that belonged to The Company. I don't see how something like that can go unpunished."

"But—"

"Hold still," says Dr. Grayson. He's standing in front of a computer monitor with his back to me. "You may feel a slight pressure around your temples." He taps a series of keys, and a machine behind me whirs to life. The metal helmet begins to pulse and warm up. Then it begins to constrict, closing tighter and tighter around my skull.

"Um . . . excuse me?" I say, trying to get Dr. Grayson's attention. The "slight pressure" feels like something crushing my cranium, like I'm in the trash compactor on the Death Star. It doesn't hurt, but it definitely doesn't feel good. I'm pretty sure that whatever is left of my human brain will liquefy and come dripping out my ears at any moment.

"Stop!" I cry, grabbing the helmet and trying in vain to pry it off my head.

"Soon," says Dr. Vogel calmly. "The scan won't last long. This is the worst of it."

Dr. Grayson keeps his eyes trained on the screen, which shows a squiggly black-and-white image that I guess is my brain. He and Dr. Vogel bend their heads together, pointing to this and that as I writhe behind them. I try to make out what they're saying, but the implosion of my head makes it difficult to eavesdrop. *Enable quadrant five. Deterioration of the anterior piston. Set phasers to stun . . .* No, that can't be right.

The scan only lasts a few minutes, but it feels like an eternity. When the helmet is finally removed, I collapse onto the table and cradle my head. As the throbbing slows down, I think maybe I am being a little dramatic. The crushing pressure wasn't *that* bad.

But then Grayson wheels over a tray loaded with items that look practically medieval—clamps and pincers and a mallet and . . . is that a handsaw?

"Um, what's that for?" I ask.

"That's for the procedure," says Dr. Vogel. "*Now* we can begin."

CHAPTER 35

Brick

HOPEWELL DROUGHT ESCALATED TO SEVERE says the graphic on the TV screen. Above it, news anchors have been blathering for fifteen minutes about dust storms and water restrictions and dying crops. But not a word about the intensified static electricity in the air. Or how it might impact someone with a fragile synthetic brain.

I check my phone again. No response from Trex. I send another message: "Still here. Leaving soon, I promise :-)." A quick stop at the diner to quit my job and hand in my uniform has turned into covering a few tables for Francie, who's still out sick. Or so she says. Maybe Brick the Spy should pay her a visit.

I don't expect Trex to text back. He's going to make me pay for pulling him out of Hopewell, at least until I tell him the truth. Which I've vowed to do tomorrow, on the drive out of town. Assuming I don't chicken out again.

"Excuse me?" asks a man seated at the counter, holding out an empty mug.

"Oh . . . sorry," I say. I slide my phone back into the pocket of my apron and refill his coffee.

"Wild weather we're having," he says, and I wince. I can't stop thinking about Allan and how "wild weather" like this probably killed him. As I suspected, there *were* lightning strikes in Winnemucca on the night of Allan's death, even though it wasn't raining. Three reports of dry lightning.

And that's not all. Lightning is normally caused by a negative charge in the clouds reaching out for a positive charge on the earth's surface. But in rare cases, it's possible for the opposite to occur—positive ions at the top of a thundercloud zapping a negative charge on the ground. And Allan was teeming with electrons.

Dry lightning. Positive lightning. What are the odds of both rare phenomena occurring at once?

And what are the odds of it happening twice? I don't have the slightest idea, but I'm not willing to find out. After all, what's lightning but a giant burst of static electricity—the very thing we feared? The very thing brewing in the atmosphere above Hopewell. Just my luck to settle in a place where the air itself is the biggest threat.

I look back at the TV, and my eyes go glassy. In a few hours, we'll have disappeared to someplace rainy. Someplace with floods. Heck, I'd take a tsunami over any kind of lightning.

There's only one silver lining to this whole situation—at least I know The Company's not involved. For once, it's not Kellerman Vogel I'm afraid of. He's good, but even he can't control the weather.

CHAPTER 36

Mellie

"Five milligrams!" roars Mack. "How do you confuse five milligrams and point five milligrams, you worthless sack of beef jerky?"

"Numbers aren't really my strong suit," says Lou. He hangs his head and looks almost small. "You're the scientist. Why didn't *you* measure the tranquilizer?"

I think Lou makes a solid point, but nobody's asking for my opinion.

Mack groans and turns to me, jiggling the empty can of ginger ale. "You really drank this whole thing?"

I burp.

"That ain't good," whimpers Lou, shaking his head.

"Of course it ain't good!" snaps Mack.

"What did you give me?" I mumble. Whatever it is, I can feel it working, like fingertips smudging everything in sight, turning my world into an impressionist painting. The goons aren't so scary when they're just dabs of color. "Did you give me these?" I squint at the label on the orange pill bottle on the desk, but the letters squirm and wiggle.

"Those things are Tic Tacs compared to what we gave you," says Lou. "You just drank enough tranquilizers to take down a horse!"

"Shut it!" barks Mack, fiercely pacing the room. "The boss wanted her to be docile. Not . . . this." I am waving my fingers in front of my face. They leave a trail in the air, like lit sparklers.

The goons move to a far corner of the room and huddle together, whispering and glancing over at me every once in a while. They look nervous. Maybe they're beginning to realize who they're up against.

But my mind is leaving, traveling up, up, up, like I'm on a rocket ship blasting away from this horrible place to somewhere black and quiet and full of stars.

No, I tell myself. I can't fly away. I have to stay. I have to find Trex. I have to tell him the truth about these people.

Stay, Mellie.

But I can't let on that I'm still here, watching. I have to hide, inside myself.

I'm good at hiding.

I hide in my room mostly. I see things from up there. Like the time I saw that boy get shocked by a statue. Or did he shock the statue? Who was that boy?

I feel myself slipping away. *Come back, Mellie. Stay.*

Trex

"We're just going to take a few samples," says Dr. Vogel. I don't even want to think about what he's planning to take samples of, and I don't intend to find out.

"It's been a long day," I say, pretending to yawn. "Discovering my whole life is a lie has really worn me out. Why don't we pick this up in the morning, when we've all had a chance to recharge?" At that, I place my lucky baseball cap back on my head. I instantly feel better.

"We've been waiting eight years for this," says Dr. Vogel.

"Exactly," I say. "What's a few more hours?"

"We'll take the samples *now*," he says. All the awkwardness of that initial greeting is gone from his demeanor. He's like a different person. And this version is kind of a jerk. "Grayson, continue the preparations."

"No!" I say, scooting along the table, away from the doctor.

Dr. Vogel takes a deep breath and massages the bridge of his nose with two fingers, the way Mom does when I'm trying her patience. As angry as I am at her, I'd give anything to be curled up on the couch with her right now, playing Alphabetter. Even arguing with her would be better than this.

"This will all go much more smoothly if you cooperate," says Dr. Vogel.

"And what if I don't?"

"Let's not find out."

I seek out Dr. Grayson for backup, but he's wearing that shame-faced look that Barnaby gets when Mom and I are fighting and he doesn't want to pick a side.

"Don't you understand what we're offering you here?" says Dr. Vogel. "You'd be a fool to walk away from this. And, let's not forget, you'll also be dead."

"I'll come back," I say. "I just want to . . . I want to talk to Mom. I want to go home."

"All right," says Dr. Vogel, steadying himself with a deep breath. "If that's the way we're going to do this, so be it. I've been indulging you so far, hoping you'd listen to reason and work with us voluntarily. But it seems you're as stubborn as that woman. The truth is, you don't exactly have a choice in the matter. After your parents died, The Company was granted legal authority to make medical decisions on your behalf. So technically, I'm the closest thing you have to a parent. And I'm telling you—we're doing this *now*."

He stares at me, and he's transformed. His jaw is set. His eyes are steely. I liked him much better when he was a gawky science nerd. I feel like I've stepped back into the horror movie. Why didn't I listen to Mellie? Or Mom? Or any of the imaginary audience members who could've easily predicted all this?

"Grayson, give him the good stuff," says Dr. Vogel.

"Uh . . . yes, sir." Dr. Grayson fumbles with the instruments on the tray. His trembling fingers aren't making me feel any better, especially when he lifts a syringe you'd use to give shots to Bigfoot.

"No!" I shout.

In two long strides, Dr. Vogel is over me, holding my arms flat against my sides. His scrawny limbs are surprisingly strong.

"I don't want to do this," I moan. "Let me go!"

Dr. Grayson aims the syringe at my left forearm. I assume it contains a powerful sedative. If that needle hits its mark, I'll be at the mercy of The Company and all the other barbaric instruments on that tray. I can't let that happen.

But like Dr. Vogel said, I don't exactly have a choice in the matter.

Mellie

I hear a commotion, a crash of metal and raised voices. For some reason, it makes me laugh again, like when people fall down on TV, their arms and legs flailing everywhere. Lou puts on pink gloves, and that also makes me laugh. He isn't amused.

"Let's check on the boss," says Mack.

"Can we leave her alone?" asks Lou.

"She's not going anywhere. Just lock the door."

Then they smile, and so do I. Only mine is on the inside. I've fooled them.

As soon as the door closes and locks, I straighten up, even though my head wobbles around like my bobblehead. I slink over to Vogel's chair and fall into it. No wonder everyone likes this chair. It's like a hug for my . . .

Focus, Mellie.

I *am* a good detective. I pay attention. When Vogel was connecting Trex to the internet, I was watching, in the dark reflection of the windowpane, memorizing every keystroke. My fingers are slow and clumsy, but I manage to type the commands. Then the password: "KellerIsTheMan123." He's just asking to get hacked with that one.

The last program he was using is still up on the screen. As far as I can tell, it's written entirely in Geek, but I make out a few lines that make sense.

Connect? I click Yes.

Restrict Access? I click No.

When I'm done, I collapse back into the squishy seat. I bounce a few times and swivel back and forth. Then I see my name on the computer screen, beneath a document titled "Melissa Chandler." I click on it.

It's a scanned form, dated over a week ago. Each line has been filled out in Dr. Colson's sloppy handwriting. That's how The Company knows about my diagnosis and medication. They hacked Dr. Colson. Of all the dirty tricks. But while I'm snooping, I might as well see what he had to say . . .

Patient: Melissa Chandler
Age: 12
Diagnosis: Generalized anxiety
disorder; panic disorder; school
avoidance

The words on the screen practically dance, snaking all over the page until they could spell out anything. Even, possibly, "gastrointestinal esophageal reflux disease." I scroll down to Dr. Colson's notes: *Patient is obviously very intelligent.* Hm, perhaps he isn't such a quack after all. I read more. *But she was inattentive and distracted during her appointment. She has been informed of her diagnosis by parents and previous physicians, but she continues to insist that the disorder is a purely physical one. She is either unable or unwilling to see the true nature of her illness.*

Excuse me?

Inattentive?

Distracted?

Unable or unwilling to see?

My eyes are my most reliable body part! Seeing is what I do. Paying attention is what I do.

I feel the tranquilizer coursing through my bloodstream, tugging at my eyelids, pulling me away. I blink hard, so the words stop prancing across the screen. I make myself look.

It's not what you look at that matters. It's what you see. Stupid Thoreau and his stupid inspirational wall sign.

I remove a crumpled brochure from my pocket. There are the smiling faces. The "normal" kids.

It says: *Living with Anxiety.* And I finally see.

CHAPTER 37

Trex

The syringe plunges into my skin, and I howl. Not because it hurts but because it means The Company has won. They've got me.

Wait. On second thought . . . it *does* hurt. I feel the pinch of the needle entering my body. How is that possible?

My arm reacts to the unfamiliar feeling by jerking away, and my legs thrash. The sudden movement knocks Dr. Grayson off balance. The syringe slips out of his hand, pinwheels through the air, and crashes on the floor. Its contents—"the good stuff"—leak out in a puddle, instead of into my veins.

Dr. Vogel loses his grip on me, too. I squirm away from him and leap off the table, toppling the tray. Instruments go flying, skittering across the floor with a tremendous clatter. I lunge for the door. I have to find Mellie and get us both out of here.

My daring escape lasts all of twenty-five seconds. I burst into the hallway only to crash face-first into a slab of concrete wearing pink rubber gloves. "Where do you think you're going?" Lou grunts at me.

"I'm going home," I say, trying to slip around him. But his bulk blocks me in.

Dr. Vogel catches up to me. "Let me make this abundantly clear," he says. "Your participation isn't optional."

"Our parents will come looking for us," I say. "You're not going to get away with this!"

"There's another thing you should know about The Company," says Dr. Vogel. "Not only do we employ the best doctors and scientists in the world, we're also staffed with the country's finest attorneys. I assure you, there's not much we can't get away with."

"That's not true! You can't just kidnap kids."

"Kidnap?" he says, pretending to be offended. "What an awful word to toss around. I'm not kidnapping anybody. I'm providing you with essential medical care that you've been deprived of by a malicious woman who did, in fact, kidnap you."

"I'll tell everyone the truth! I'll tell all about you and your evil company!"

"Ah, yes, the truth." Vogel sneers. "How quaint. Let me give you a heavy dose of the truth. This 'evil' company installed millions of dollars' worth of technology into your body, and Britt stole it from us. More than that, she robbed us of technological breakthroughs that would have saved lives and made me a billionaire in the process. For that, I intend to make her pay. And I intend to reclaim what's mine. My legacy *and* my technology."

He reaches into his pocket and removes a black box no larger than a deck of cards. It looks like a remote control with only one button.

"Not only do you lack a proper legal guardian, Trex, you also have stolen property in your body. So you have two options. You can cooperate with us and let our legal team make sure someone suitable is appointed to look after you. Or—and I shudder even to think of it—The Company can take back what belongs to us."

"What? You can't mean—"

"Yes, Trex. That's exactly what I mean. Your technology can easily be extracted."

"Nobody would ever let you do that!"

"Maybe not," he says. "But maybe. Do you want to find out?"

"Mom was right about you," I say. "Mom was . . . right." The truth of that statement hits me like a punch to the gut. That's why she took me—because she knew Vogel was evil. She was trying to rescue me from him. *She's* the one who saved me. "You—" I snap at Vogel. "*You* planted messages in my brain to make me hate her."

"I merely furnished you with the truth, Trex. You took it upon yourself to hate her."

"But you didn't give me the whole story. I should've talked to her first. I should've asked her . . ."

"It's a little late for that, isn't it?" smirks Dr. Vogel. "You're here now. And you belong to The Company. The sooner you accept that, the easier this will be on everyone. Now, please, let the grown-ups talk." He turns to Mack. "Is the girl ready?"

"Yes, sir," says Mack.

"Excellent. Lou, keep an eye on this one." He tosses Lou the little black box. "This will keep him in line. Now that we've reactivated his pain receptors, I'm sure he'll be much more cooperative." He gives me a wry smile. "Dr. Grayson, please tidy up the exam room. We'll be needing it again shortly. Mack and I are going to attend to the girl now."

"Leave Mellie alone!" I croak. "She's got nothing to do with this!"

"Rest assured," says Dr. Vogel, "I intend to take care of you both."

A surge of blind anger propels me forward. I lunge at him with my hands curled into claws, stretching for his throat. Jolts of electricity leap from my fingers. But something stops me before I can reach him.

An intense pain starts at the back of my head and shoots down my spine. The same thing I felt in my room right before the visions started. Lou is pressing down on the button on the little black box.

I shrivel up in anguish, but Lou's trigger finger wasn't quite fast enough. Dr. Vogel is moaning, too, his hands wrapped around his neck. When he releases them, he reveals red burns in the shape of my fingers, marking his skin. Through the fog of my own pain, I smile.

CHAPTER 38

Brick

What compels a woman with no family, no friends, no *life*, to up and steal a little boy? Trust me, I've been wondering that myself. For the last eight years.

I wasn't equipped to become a mother the night I took Trex, and for the first time in my life, I didn't have a plan. I just knew I had to get him out of there.

I didn't know what sort of security Vogel had installed in the lab, so I stepped outside to call Ronnie. "Are you still seeing that No-Good Boyfriend?" I asked.

"If you'd only get to know him—" she began, but I cut her off.

"Can he get documents? Fake IDs, birth certificates, that sort of thing?" I sounded like a stranger to myself. I was someone who followed the rules. I did what I was told. I certainly didn't kidnap children. I wasn't even a kid person. I'd always preferred dogs.

"Probably, but . . . what's going on, Brick? Are you in trouble?"

"Not yet," I said. "But I'm about to be."

Trex was still inside, strung up to a bunch of machines. Getting him out wouldn't be easy. In fact, it would be nearly impossible for anyone who didn't understand what The Company had done to him. I sat down on a cold stone bench to go over the logistics. It would never work. But it *had* to work. If I was going to sacrifice my career and my freedom for this kid, it had to work.

I slumped forward, my head cradled in my hands, my body heavy with the weight of what I was about to do. I was about to leave everything behind and plunge headfirst into a life I wasn't prepared for. I was about to sink. Just like a brick.

CHAPTER 39

Mellie

By the time the bad guys come back, I'm slouched over in my seat, right where they left me. Dr. Vogel's computer screen is black. They'll never know what I did while they were gone.

Suckers.

I try to lift my head when they enter, but now that I've let it droop, I realize how heavy it is. Has it always been this heavy? It's like a pumpkin. Or a bowling ball.

The boy with hollow bones is with them, being dragged along.

What's his name again?

T. rex?

What's he doing here?

What am *I* doing here?

"What have you done to her?" asks T. rex. I can tell he's worried. About me.

"She's fine," says Vogel. Something has burned his neck. The skin is tender and red and beginning to blister. Lightning Boy strikes again!

"I'm fine," I chant. "Fine, fine, fine."

"We have to get her home," says Lightning Boy. "Or to a hospital."

"We'll fix her right up," says Vogel.

Something tells me he doesn't mean it. My detective skills are still working! Mack grabs me by the wrist and pulls me toward the door. "Out you go, Looney Tunes."

"She's not crazy!" says Lightning Boy. "You did something to her!"

Lou shoves Lightning Boy into the room, into the chair I just left.

"Say goodbye to your friend," Mack whispers to me.

"Friend," I say. Now I remember. That's Trex. He's my friend. My only friend.

"Mellie, I'll get you out of this," he says.

"I know you will," I say, stumbling away from my captor and toward Trex. "Because you're a superhero. You're Lightning Boy!"

Trex

"Lightning Boy?" chuckles Lou after they've pulled Mellie out of the room. "Pretty fancy name for a pipsqueak."

"Nice gloves," I shoot back.

He glances down at his pink rubber gardening gloves, as if he forgot he was wearing them, then sneers at me. "The fists inside them work just fine."

I don't challenge him. It has become abundantly clear that my pain receptors are working perfectly after all this time. Even now, with nobody actively hurting me, my body aches from where they hurt me before. If this is what it feels like to be normal, maybe I should rethink my goals in life.

"I hate to break it to you," says Lou, "but sometimes you're the lightning, and sometimes you're the rod. Today, you're the rod, kid."

"Did you read that on a bumper sticker?" I say.

The big oaf is probably right, but I'm not ready to give up yet. I think back to all the kidnap scenes I've seen on TV. The kidnappee always tries to get the captor talking. It distracts them and sometimes even gets them to reveal something important. Especially someone as thick as this guy.

"So . . . I detect an accent," I say, trying to sound all casual. "Are you from New York?"

"Ha!" barks Lou. "Nice try, kid. Did you really think that would work on me? Are you from . . . Idiotville or something?"

"No, but did you know that Idiotville is a real town? It's in Oregon. Tillamook County. Fifty miles northwest of Portland."

"Huh?"

Yeah . . . *huh*? How do I know that?

"Ask me a question," I blurt out.

"What are you talking about? If this is some sort of trick—" says Lou.

"A math problem. Ask me a math problem!" I insist.

"Uh . . . okay. What's two plus two?"

"No, a *hard* math problem."

"Uh . . . what's a billion times a billion?"

"A quintillion," I reply, a grin overtaking my face. I've never heard that word before in my life, but I say it again, just to savor the sound. "A quintillion!"

Lou rolls his eyes. "You're as bonkers as your friend."

"Thank you."

Like I said, get your captor talking. Lou doesn't know it, but he just gave me the upper hand. His lame Idiotville joke revealed that I'm back online. But how?

Then I realize that Mellie was left alone in Vogel's office with only Lou and Mack to guard her. I have a sneaking suspicion she was able to outsmart those two with her eyes closed.

Lou has also reminded me that I have two options—I can sit around waiting to get hit by lightning, or I can strike first. And I intend to do the striking.

If these guys are going to mess with my brain, my brain is going to mess with them right back.

Mellie

"What's the plan?" asks Mack.

"Yeah, what's the plan?" I echo.

Mack yanks me by the arm through the rat's maze of the building. I count the doors we pass—*one, two, three, four, five*—or maybe it's just one door multiplied by my blurry eyes. They used to be my most reliable body part, but I don't trust them anymore.

A door slams, and we're outside. It's all trees and dirt and rocks and not much else. The sky is strange today. Alive, in a way. I wonder if it's going to rain at last.

We forge ahead, deeper into the brush. Mack and Vogel walk on either side of me, gripping my forearms. Branches reach out and clutch at our clothes. It's like something out of a fairy tale. One of the scary ones.

"The girl is going to have an accident," Vogel explains. "Off Company property, of course."

He says it as though I'm not there listening. Then I

remember that I'm still hiding in plain sight. Incognito. Doing what detectives do best.

"The kids came snooping around back here," says Vogel. "They like to play detective. Isn't that what the snitch told you?"

"That's right, boss," says Mack, pulling me along beside him. "He said she's always spying on everyone. Thinks she's a regular Sherlock Holmes."

I picture Harrison's smug, glowing face and wish I could smash a snickerdoodle into it.

"The girl was poking around where she shouldn't have been," says Vogel, "and she lost her footing, took a nasty spill, and hit her head. Simple as that." Vogel lays out his evil plan casually, as if he's giving directions to the drugstore. *Make a left at the stop sign, a right at the McDonald's, push a kid off a cliff . . .*

"Brilliant," says Mack.

I have to admit it is a pretty good plan, in my professional opinion. If only it didn't involve the collision of my head with the rocky bottom of a ditch.

I giggle at the term "rocky bottom." I'm not scared, thanks to whatever the goons put in my ginger ale.

When Mack's not paying attention, I reach down and pinch myself on the thigh. Not to confirm whether this is real—even through the gauzy lens of the tranquilizers, I know it's real. I pinch myself to see if I can still feel. I want to know how much this is going to hurt.

CHAPTER 40

Trex

To: hopewellpd@hopewell.gov
From: trex.wilson@botmail.com
Subject: HELP!

To Whom It May Concern,

My friend, Melissa Chandler, and I have been kidnapped by Dr. Kellerman Vogel III of The Human Engineering Company. We are being held at 1801 Baumgarten Boulevard. This is not a joke! Send help immediately!

Sincerely,
Trex Wilson

I see the words in my head, as if I've typed them on a screen. But all I have to do is think them, and they appear, floating behind my eyes. I cast around for the Send button, and there it is, a bright red rectangle in my mind. I think about clicking it and instantly hear a whooshing sound, like the message is flying off into cyberspace.

We'll be rescued for sure.

Ping. A happy little beep announces an incoming email. The message pops up in my head from out of nowhere.

To: trex.wilson@botmail.com
From: hopewellpd@hopewell.gov
Subject: UNDELIVERABLE: HELP!

Ugh.

"What are you doing?" barks Lou. His voice pulls me out of my head and back into Dr. Vogel's office. My eyes are closed, but I can feel his face inches away from mine. His breath smells like deli meat.

"Just resting my eyes," I say. Definitely not scheming my escape. Or searching the internet. Or sending urgent emails to everyone I can think of.

Hopewell Hill Police Department?

Check.

Federal Bureau of Investigation?

Check.

I even sent a message to the chat room in *Legends of Oren*.

But all my messages are bouncing back or going unanswered. I mean, who'd believe my story anyway? An evil CEO has me trapped in an abandoned warehouse so he can pry into my synthetic brain? Yeah, right.

"Wake up!" barks Lou, snapping his fingers millimeters from the end of my nose.

Well, if he insists . . .

My eyes spring open. "Louis Gumperson!"

"Excuse me?"

"You don't strike me as a Gumperson," I say.

"I'll strike you right now if you don't shut up," says Lou. His droopy face grows red and animated, exactly the reaction I was hoping for. "How do you know my name?"

"I've got a computer brain, remember?"

"No way. That's not real."

"You're Louis Gumperson. Thirty-two years old. Born in Brooklyn. Lives at 22-B Winchester Street."

"No way!" breathes Lou, backing away from me like I might bite him. "What else can you see?"

I close my eyes again. I focus on Lou. "You live with . . . your mother? Really?"

"She has a rent-controlled apartment," he says sheepishly.

"Bernice seems like a sweet lady."

"You can see Mimi?"

"Yep. It says here she makes prize-winning . . ." I gasp. "Snickerdoodles! Did you let Mack use Mimi's famous cookies to lure children into the clutches of The Company?"

"Uhhh . . ."

"Does Bernice know what you do for a living?"

"Of course she does," he says. "She tells all her friends I got a fancy corporate job."

"She knows you work for The Company. But does she know what you *do* for The Company?"

"Uhhh . . ."

"Did they tell you I can take pictures?" I ask. "And videos? Just by looking at something. It's another one of my abilities." It's not true—at least not that I know of—but it does the trick.

"So what?" says Lou, his cleft chin quaking.

"What if I told you I've been recording you all day? It sure would be a shame if that footage wound up in Bernice's inbox, wouldn't it?"

"Mimi doesn't know how to open an email without my help," says Lou. "So there."

"I thought that might be the case. That's why I'm sending the file to everyone in her building, too. Mr. Cooper across the hall, with the cats. The Chin family next door. Oh, I see that Mr. Chin is the landlord. I hope the video doesn't upset him. It would be a real shame if you two got evicted. Bye-bye, rent control."

"Are you threatening me?" scowls Lou. He stomps back over to me, his muscled chest heaving. I can tell his every instinct is driving him to hit me.

"Careful," I say, bracing myself for the impact of those massive clenched fists with my jaw. "You're on video."

—⚡—

Mellie

Trees and dirt and rocks.

Trees and dirt and rocks.

People are always going on and on about the stunning variety of nature, but it seems pretty monotonous to me. "Do you really know where we're going?" I ask the bad guys. We've been walking for what seems like forever, and I'm convinced we've gone in a giant circle. I guess it serves them right for drugging the one person among us with exceptional navigation skills.

"Pipe down," says Mack. "You're not exactly in a position to be questioning our methods here."

"I'll have you know I have exceptional navigation skills," I say. "I'm like a walking nap."

"Nap?" says Mack.

"I mean nap."

"You said nap again."

"No. With the streets and stuff. Naps."

"Maps?"

"Yes, naps," I say. "Can I lie down?"

My knees don't wait for permission. I sink into the pine needles beneath me, dragging Mack's left arm down with me.

"You've got to be kidding," he says.

"Well . . . ," says Vogel impatiently, "she's not going to carry herself."

Suddenly, I'm floating. It reminds me of car rides back from the baseball stadium, after night games. I'd always fall asleep in the back seat with my face squished against the windowpane, and Father would carry me inside. So far above the ground but somehow safe.

For a brief moment, I nuzzle into Mack's collar. Then I remember he wants to kill me. And he smells like spinach.

"She's drooling on me!" he says. "Gross!"

"Shut up!" snaps Vogel. "We're nearly there. You're going to have to carry her back, too, and she'll probably be bloody."

"I'm sending The Company my dry-cleaning bill," mutters Mack.

"What?" asks Vogel.

"Nothing," says Mack.

We walk a bit farther, the steady crunch of leaves

soothing me like a lullaby. Then Vogel yells "Stop!" and the song comes to an end. "Another step and we'll all be in the ravine." I hear skittering pebbles falling down, down, down.

An enormous clap of thunder reverberates through the sky. But not a drop of rain.

The next part happens quickly. I try to stop it, but my body is moving from the inside out, rejecting whatever was in that ginger ale. I spew it all back out onto the most appropriate target.

"Argggggghhhh!" roars Mack, almost dropping me. "She puked on me!" A thick, vile liquid drips down my chin onto the front of his polo shirt.

"Get over it," says Vogel. "We've got more important things to worry about."

"I am definitely sending The Company my dry-cleaning bill," Mack murmurs.

"Excuse me?" asks Vogel, with a single raised eyebrow.

"Nothing, boss."

"Good. If you're quite through worrying about your clothing, let's get on with it. Throw her in."

CHAPTER 41

Brick

With my final paycheck in hand, I walk out the glass doors of the diner for the last time. I won't miss the Plate of the Union Café, especially the awful suspenders and the sparkly bow tie that cost me $15.99. What I wouldn't give for a long, pristine lab coat. But alas, my lab coat days are far behind me.

The sky above is a weird metallic gray, and a bank of ominous clouds shrouds the sun. Maybe the people on TV were wrong. Maybe it's going to rain in Hopewell after all. The drought increases the electricity in the air, but the clouds bring lightning. It seems we can't win.

"Excuse me, ma'am."

I'm so preoccupied that I don't notice the police officer standing in front of me, blocking the way to my car. My heart races, and I begin to shake so hard my keys jingle in my hand. I always expected The Company to send back-alley criminals after me. Vogel is too shady to contact the police. Did someone else find out what I did all those years ago? Does it end here, in the parking lot of this cheesy diner? Will I get to say goodbye to Trex?

A boy with shiny red cheeks steps out from behind the officer. I recognize him from the neighborhood. Harrison, the obnoxious one. He's cradling his arm. The skin there is pink and rippled, with a jagged burn mark snaking along his forearm.

Oh, Trex, what have you done?

CHAPTER 42

Trex

"What are they going to do to Mellie?" I ask.

Lou squirms under my gaze. He stares into my eyes like he might actually be able to see the hidden camera there. "The boss said he's gonna bring her out back and 'take care of her.' I don't think he's planning to give her chicken soup."

"Wait, are you saying . . . are they going to *kill* Mellie?"

"Seems that way," says Lou. "But what do I know? I've got a normal puny brain."

"Why would they do that? What does Mellie have to do with this?"

"Nothin'." Lou shrugs. "She just knows too much. The boss hates loose ends. That's why he's been chasing you and Brick all these years."

So that's what Mellie is now—a loose end to be

snipped off. And all because I wanted to be normal at any cost. All because I wasn't honest with Mom, and she wasn't honest with me. Now Mellie will pay the price. Guilt and fear and anger claw at me.

"That's not gonna help," says Lou, nodding at my bluish fingers. "If you wanna save your friend, you'd better keep your cool." He smiles and tilts his head, and I realize he's posing for my imaginary camera. I guess he's playing the good guy now, for Mimi's sake. I can use this to my advantage.

"What do I have to do to save Mellie?" I ask.

"Delete any videos you got of me . . . working," he says, "and I'll get you out of here."

"Deal," I say.

Lou opens the door of Dr. Vogel's office and peers both ways before waving me over. He nudges me out ahead of him, and I walk down the hall with my head down, like a prisoner. He waves the black box around and makes loud, over-the-top threats, even though the halls are empty. "Don't make me press this button! I'll do it! Don't test me!"

He finally shoves me toward a set of double doors at the end of the hallway. "That leads out back," he whispers. "You're on your own from here."

"Thanks," I say. I push open the door.

"Er, excuse me!" a voice calls out behind us. "Where do you think you're going?"

I stop in my tracks and turn. Dr. Grayson is speed-walking toward us, holding a clipboard in one hand and a walkie-talkie in the other. He's trying to keep it together, but he visibly gulps when Lou steps up to him.

"The boss wants to see the kid," says Lou.

"Out there?"

"Yeah."

"That's highly unusual," says Dr. Grayson. He raises the walkie-talkie to his lips. "Let me just confirm—"

"That won't be necessary," says Lou. He plucks the device from Dr. Grayson's hand, while the doctor looks on helplessly. Then, with his thumb, Lou presses on the antenna until it snaps in half. He hands the walkie-talkie back to the doctor, with its antenna dangling from a few thin copper wires. Dr. Grayson tucks the mangled device into the pocket of his lab coat, as if nothing is wrong with it. "Um . . . er . . . all right, then," he mumbles, pale with fear. "Carry on." He turns on his heel and practically runs off down the hallway.

"You'd better go," I say to Lou. "You don't want to be another of The Company's loose ends."

"Lou Gumperson can take care of himself," says Lou, puffing out his already-puffy chest—another performance for the camera. Then he squeezes the black box in his hand until the plastic casing pops off and the delicate innards spill out onto the floor.

"Thanks," I say. "And can I ask one more favor?"

"Don't push it, kid. Whaddaya want?"

"Can I borrow your gloves?"

Mellie

I have dreams about flying. Most of the time, I'm soaring over Hopewell Hill, looking down at the rooftops. Then through them, at the people inside. I want to peek into their lives, just for a moment. To know them. To understand them. Spying seems like the only way.

Tonight, I will fly for real, but the only thing beneath me will be rock.

"Me?" gulps Mack, still cradling me like an oversized baby. "You want *me* to throw her in? I thought . . ."

"You thought what?" barks Vogel. "You thought the CEO of a multimillion-dollar company was going to throw a girl into a ravine?"

"B-but I'm head of software engineering!"

"And I'm head of *everything*," sighs Vogel, rolling his eyes to the pitching sky.

"Well, when you put it that way." Mack hesitates. "Sir?"

"What is it?"

"Are you looking for an actual toss? Or more of a drop?"

"Ugh. I don't care how you do it, you idiot. Just make sure the job is done."

"So maybe a sort of roll?"

"Yes. A roll. Get on with it."

But here's what they don't know—now that I've regurgitated all those tranquilizers, I'm coming back to my senses. Floating merrily toward an imminent death is no longer acceptable. A good detective doesn't give up when the chips are down—not when she has an ounce of energy left. Summoning every bit of it, I swing my arm in a wide arc and whack Mack on the side of the face. I'm clumsy and weak, but I have one thing going for me—the element of surprise. I catch him off guard and hop out of his arms.

But I'm still slow. So very slow. Mack grabs me again easily, seizing me by the wrist and jerking me toward the ravine. My attempt to save myself has made him angry and wiped out his last bit of hesitation about murdering me. I can feel the ledge beneath my shoes where the solid ground comes to an abrupt end. I peer down, but it's shadowy and dark. I have no idea how long I'll fall before I make contact. I feel like puking again, but there's nothing left in me. My body heaves. Mack's hand presses into the small of my back, pushing me forward.

"Leave her alone!" cries someone behind us.

Mack looks over his shoulder, and so do I.

I see an outline of Trex—the vaguest idea of Trex. I'm probably dreaming or hallucinating still, but I swear he's standing there between two trees, with his hands on his hips and his legs planted wide. In the unmistakable pose of a superhero.

Trex

"Leave her alone!" I cry out. I'm standing in a clearing by the ravine, wearing Lou's pink rubber gloves. "I'm the one you want."

"You're right," says Dr. Vogel. "But the girl is involved now. And whose fault is that?"

"It's mine," I say, "and I'm sorry." The apology is directed at Mellie. I'm not sure whether she can hear or understand me, but I say it all the same.

"It's too late for an apology," says Dr. Vogel.

"She won't tell anyone!" I shout. "Mellie is good at keeping secrets. It's what she does best. Let her go, and I'll come with you, willingly."

"Fabulous idea," says Dr. Vogel. "I'll stake my company and my reputation on the word of a couple of twelve-year-olds."

"Then blackmail her," I say. "Bribe her. Threaten everyone she knows and loves. Just don't hurt her."

"I remain disappointed in you, Trex. For all the computing power in your head, you still don't get it," says Vogel. "Don't you see—"

A high-pitched wail rises up over the trees. A siren.

"What's that?" Vogel asks. His eyes dart to Mack,

who shrugs. Vogel shouts into his walkie-talkie, "Grayson, what's going on?"

Thanks to Lou, he gets nothing but static in response. The wailing is getting louder. Closer. We all turn toward the building in the distance. Through the trees I can make out the flashing of lights. Red and blue. The police. We're saved!

"Oh no," groans Mack, still gripping Mellie by the arm. "What do we do?"

"Grayson!" roars Dr. Vogel. "I need an update this instant! Are there police in the area?"

More static.

Then Dr. Vogel charges at me, his long legs closing the distance between us before I have time to react. He grabs my forearm, careful to wrap his fingers around my glove instead of my skin. "Did you contact them? What did you tell them?"

"I—I didn't," I stammer. "I didn't tell the police anything." It's nearly true. All my attempts to communicate with law enforcement came up empty. Undeliverable. But someone out there must have received my messages.

"New plan," Vogel says to Mack, and for the first time, I detect fear in his voice. "Throw her in. Now."

"No!" I cry.

I don't see Mellie fall. She's just not there anymore. Mack stands alone where, a second ago, there had been two people. He looks as stunned as anyone that he's actually done it. Mellie gasps once on the way down but doesn't scream. I hear a sickening crunch, a thud, and then silence.

I lunge toward the ravine, but Vogel still has his hand clamped on my arm. He pulls me back. Then, in a sudden change of heart, he drags me to the edge and pushes me in after her.

CHAPTER 43

Brick

We arrive at an abandoned, boarded-up warehouse. Our cars—mine and the police cruiser—are the only ones in the parking lot.

"Are you messing with us, kid?" barks Officer Briscoe, the cop who scared me out of my wits outside the café.

"No," says Harrison, but he looks uncharacteristically unsure of himself. "This is the address I got. 1801 Baumgarten Boulevard."

We cluster in the darkened doorway—Mrs. Chandler, Harrison Palmer, and me—while Officer Briscoe presses the buzzer. I can tell by the way he's already preparing to leave that he doesn't expect anyone to answer. He thinks Harrison's story is absurd. But he doesn't know The Company. Just as he's turning to go, the door clicks. A flustered man with a clipboard, wearing a doctor's coat, stands on the other side. "Um, can I help you?"

"I hope so," says Officer Briscoe. "We received some unusual reports regarding this address. Do you mind if we come inside?" Officer Briscoe is tall, broad-shouldered, and intimidating. He towers over the doctor, who fumbles with a walkie-talkie that seems to have been snapped in half.

"I'm not quite sure," mumbles the doctor. "I need to consult with—"

"Let them in," says a breathless voice in the background. It's meek and menacing at the same time, and my stomach does a somersault when I hear it.

"And you are . . . ?" asks Officer Briscoe.

"Kellerman Vogel III," says the man. "CEO and president of The Human Engineering Company." His head is bowed, and he fidgets like he's uncomfortable in his own skin. But it's all an act. He knows what he's doing, and so do I. "What can I do for you folks?" He scans the rest of us huddled behind the officer. His eyes spark with gleeful recognition when they land on me. I instinctively back away.

"I apologize for the inconvenience," says Officer Briscoe. "Two kids went missing this afternoon, and we received a tip leading us to this location."

"Tip?" asks an old man shoving in beside Vogel. He has a bright yellow stain on his polo shirt and smells like bile. "What sort of tip?"

"Er, this is my associate, Stewart Mackenzie," says Vogel. "Head of software engineering."

"Hey, I know you!" Harrison blurts out. "You're the dude who gave me cookies!"

"That's right," says Mack. "I'm thinking about buying a house on Hopewell Hill, since I'm relocating to this new office." He must be one of Vogel's new spies. Clever choice. Nobody would ever suspect a smelly old guy.

"If we could just take a quick look around," says Officer Briscoe.

"Of course," says Vogel, ushering us inside with a plastered-on smile. He leads us down low-lit hallways lined with empty offices. "I'm afraid we won't be much assistance in your investigation. As you can see, we're just moving into this new space. We decided to burn the midnight oil to get this equipment unpacked."

"We appreciate your cooperation," says Officer Briscoe, with infuriating deference. "We'll get out of your hair as quickly as we can."

"Now what about this tip you received?" asks Vogel.

"Yes," says Officer Briscoe, flipping through his notes. "Two kids have gone missing in the Hopewell area. Trex Wilson and Melissa Chandler. We normally don't follow up on missing persons cases until they've been gone for twenty-four hours, but the circumstances here are a bit unusual. It seems that—"

"I got a message in *Legends of Oren*," Harrison blurts out. "Not that I even play that game. Because it's super lame. But I happened to be playing today, and I saw a message from Trex Wilson saying he and Mellie

Chandler got kidnapped and were at this address. It was so weird."

Vogel half chuckles, half sighs. "Officer, with all due respect, this is obviously some sort of prank. The supposedly missing children are playing a joke on their friend here—"

"They're *not* my friends," says Harrison. "And it's not a joke. Trex wouldn't do that."

"I'm obligated to follow up on this lead," says Officer Briscoe, "no matter how bizarre it may seem. Is there any reason these kids might know about your company or this particular address?"

"No, I can't imagine how—" Vogel pauses. He scratches his smooth chin, which looks incapable of producing facial hair. "Actually, now that you mention it, the boy's name *does* sound familiar. Trex Wilson, right? Yes, I remember now. He received one of our implants many years ago."

He shoots me a knowing look. Or is it a warning look? He's daring me to speak up and tell these people everything. He knows I won't. "I believe Trex contacted Ronnie, my secretary. He had some questions about his technology. I agreed to speak with him, but I never heard from him again. He certainly never came to this facility. We'd never dream of inviting children into this space. To bring a child here, why . . . it'd be extremely dangerous."

At this, he catches my eye.

And smiles.

CHAPTER 44

Trex

I tumble down, head over feet, in a blur of dirt and falling rock. I grasp at the sides of the ravine, but it crumbles under my fingertips. I finally roll to a stop at the bottom of a deep pit—about ten feet down, I'd guess. I stand up slowly. My head feels woozy, but something else sends me reeling, something that's becoming more and more familiar. Pain. It radiates through my legs, arms, back, chest—each body part taking turns aching.

But I have to keep going. I have to find Mellie. I call her name, but she doesn't respond. I recall with a shudder the crunch and the thud I heard when she was thrown in. The possibility that I'll find her limp and lifeless is worse than any physical pain. It's pitch-black down here. The trees provide a thick canopy of leaves, and above that, the sky is like a solid slab of metal. I walk the length of the ravine, squinting to distinguish the shape of rocks from the figure of a girl. Eventually my shoe bumps against something softer than stone, and it releases a soft moan. I crouch beside Mellie and whisper to her, but she only murmurs back. Through the purplish haze, I make out a gash on her forehead—baseball-sized and oozing blood.

She's barely conscious, but she's alive.

I can still save her.

The police are here, near enough that the flash of red and blue light filters through the trees. Something I did worked, some message was received. So maybe I can do it again. I close my eyes and focus. But the darkness in my head is complete this time. Dr. Vogel must have disconnected me as soon as he realized I was back online. So I scream instead, until my throat is raw. But we're at least a half mile from the building. Help is so close, but there's nothing I can do to reach them.

I try scrambling up the side of the ravine, but I keep sliding back down and landing face-first in the dirt. It goes on like this until my legs throb and my arms sag like limp pasta noodles. The air down here is earthy and close, and I feel like I'm choking on it.

I'm frustrated and fizzing with anger. But I shove it down and try again. For Mellie.

"I'm sorry," I tell her. "I guess I'm ordinary after all."

CHAPTER 45

Brick

We trudge the endless hallways of the labyrinthine building and search the empty rooms, even the locked ones. No Trex. No Mellie. No evidence they were ever here. Slowly and reluctantly, we work our way back to the entrance of the building. Mrs. Chandler and I are arm in arm, supporting each other's weight.

"We see this all the time," Officer Briscoe tells us. "Kids run off when they get mad at their parents. But they always show up the next day when their cell phones die. Trust me."

Mrs. Chandler and I glare at him.

"So that's it?" I say. "That's all we can do?"

"I'm afraid so," says Officer Briscoe. "Dr. Vogel was kind enough to let us in here voluntarily. Anything else will require a search warrant, and a message in a video game isn't going to convince a judge to give us one. I suggest you wait at home for your children. I'm sure they'll be back any minute now."

Vogel pulls open the heavy front door and waves us through. He nods as the others pass him, but when I walk by, he steps into my path. Just a little, just enough to stop me. "It's good to see you again," he says, with an oily smile. I try to push past him, but he stretches an arm across the doorway, trapping me there. "Don't worry, Brick. Your secret is safe with me."

After all these years, this man still turns my blood to ice water. He knows he can take everything I have—my money, my freedom, my reputation. But none of that matters if he's already taken Trex. He finally lets me pass with an infuriating wink.

"Do you two know each other?" whispers Mrs. Chandler as we step back into the balmy night air.

"It's a long story," I say. "I know him well enough to know we can't believe a word he says."

We both glance back at the door closing slowly on his face, which is half-hidden in shadow.

CHAPTER 46

Trex

I remember seeing in a movie that if someone has a head injury, you should keep them awake. So I talk to Mellie, even though there's no sign she can hear me. I tell her how I tricked Lou into letting me escape. How he lives with his mother, the snickerdoodle champ of Brooklyn. And how I've embraced the title of Lightning Boy. She'll love that.

I keep chatting away, even as her wound is seeping blood and her eyelids are fluttering. I feel helpless crouched there, rambling, while she slowly dies. Dr. Vogel and Mack are the only ones who know where we are, and they're inside, lying to the police. As much as I want to be rescued, part of me hopes the cops will leave so those goons will come back for us. They won't really leave Mellie out here to die. Will they?

It's still not raining, which makes it especially eerie

when the first bolt of lightning flashes. It streaks from cloud to cloud, like some ancient gods at war up there. My skin trembles, and all the hair on my arms rises. I feel like an exposed nerve.

Mellie takes a strangled breath. I hold her hand through my squishy rubber glove.

I still don't understand why they did this to her. Mellie doesn't have enough dirt on The Company to make her a real threat. Why try to kill her when they can just tell everyone she's crazy? Isn't that the way everyone writes her off at school? Surely it's less hassle than plotting her death. Less cruel than letting her bleed to death out here, while just inside, they've got enough medical equipment to run a whole hospital. Enough technology to save her. To take care of her.

I gasp.

Those were Vogel's exact words. He said he wanted to "take care of her." It hits me like lightning, and I begin to tremble. Vogel doesn't want to *kill* Mellie. He wants to *save* her.

She's not a loose end. She's The Company's next patient.

Because who in their right mind would volunteer to receive an experimental brain implant with a spotty rate of success? Someone on the verge of death, maybe. Someone who can't object. Someone on psychiatric drugs who shows up in penguin-print pajama pants, whose very illness can be used against her. Someone whose accident will be believable, because she's a spy and a snoop. Now Vogel has the perfect excuse to swoop in and give her the same technology he gave me. Not only will nobody blame him for slicing into her skull— they'll applaud him as a hero.

It's a brilliant plan. Evil, but brilliant.

And I wonder, with a sinking heart, whether this is the first time The Company has carried out a plan like that.

Another crackle of lightning streaks the sky.

There's still no rain in sight.

CHAPTER 47

Brick

Trex woke up three days after the car accident. He was re-covering better than anyone expected—disoriented and scared, but alive. Of course, nobody referred to him as "Trex" back then. He was always the "subject" or the "patient." None of us knew his real name. Perhaps we regarded him as more machine than person. Perhaps no-body wanted to get too attached.

I was covering the night shift when I heard the men speaking in hushed voices. I only recognized one of them—Kellerman Vogel III, CEO of The Company. The other man was an attorney in a fancy suit. They didn't know I was listening.

"Do the hospital's records confirm our position?" whispered the lawyer.

"Absolutely," said Vogel. "The boy was pronounced brain-dead in the ER and then transferred to us, where his condition only worsened. That's the official story."

"Are there any witnesses who might contradict that account?" asked the lawyer. "Did anyone see the boy awake after the accident?"

"There was another motorist at the scene," said Vogel. "He was comforting the child."

"How should I handle him?"

"Do I really have to spell everything out for you?" snapped Vogel. "The usual. Pay him. As much as it takes. And if he refuses to keep quiet, take care of it. Do you understand?"

"Y-yes, sir."

"It's your job to make sure there's only one version of events in the public record. The boy was brain-dead. The ER was unable to stabilize him without my intervention. I saved him. And then I made him better."

"Yes, sir," said the lawyer, in what was almost a whimper.

"That boy is going to thank me one day," said Vogel.

I clasped a hand over my mouth so they wouldn't hear me retch. That little boy didn't *need* that surgery or a fancy new brain. We altered him when he still had a chance to be normal. We took advantage of him when nobody was there to speak for him. We weren't heroes—as we'd been led to believe—but villains. In that moment, when I realized the part I'd played—was *still* playing—in that little boy's life, everything changed.

I didn't know what I was going to do when I heard those men whispering, but I knew I was going to do *something.* I knew I'd be the one to speak up for the boy from that day forward.

That's the day I really became Trex Wilson's mom, though neither of us knew it yet.

Since then, I've made countless mistakes, and Trex has every reason to hate me for them.

For all the lies. For all the secrets.

For not knowing the difference between the two.

CHAPTER 48

Mellie

I can't move. Can't speak. But I hear everything, and I understand. When Trex gasps, I can tell he's finally worked out The Company's evil plan. Just a few minutes after I did. Not bad, for an amateur. As soon as those men dumped me into this pit, I knew. If you're trying to kill a person, you don't drop her a mere ten feet. They were trying to wound me, at best. Once I figured that out, it was easy to piece together the rest. I'm an experiment. The next Trex. Lightning Girl.

Through my eyelashes, I catch hazy glimpses of Trex. He looks at me with guilt and pity on his face. He knows exactly what they're going to do to me. I'd like to ask him what to expect. Will I still be *me* afterward? When they swap out pieces of my brain and replace them with plastic and metal, will I still think the same thoughts?

At least if they give me a bionic brain, I won't need

doctors or pills anymore. Maybe I'll be able to walk into a crowd and not feel like all the eyes on me are angry little fists. I'll be able to face Harrison and Ridley and Ben and Danica and remain upright, instead of doubled over and scurrying home. I'll never again be the girl who pukes on someone else's birthday cake. That doesn't sound so bad, actually.

I wish I could make Trex hear me right now, in case it's my last chance. First, I'd tell him to stop trying to scale the walls of this ravine. If there's a way out of here, it's not by climbing.

Second, I'd tell him . . . everything else. All the secrets I've been keeping for so long. Not other people's secrets. Mine. About "living with anxiety" but willing it to be stomachaches. About the grown-up doctor with the fancy lobby and the scuff marks on his marble floor. About the rug in Father's office I wanted to fly away on. About the plastic cup, still sitting on my desk, empty. About being perched on a dunk tank and waiting to go under. About how collecting people's secrets is almost like knowing them, but safer. And not as good.

Above Trex, I see the sky in bursts. It's lit with fire, putting on a show. It's beautiful.

CHAPTER 49

Trex

The police are leaving. Their car engines roar to life and then fade away. The lights stop flashing.

But they *can't* be leaving. They were here to rescue us. The big finale. The happy ending. If they leave, then nobody is going to save us. This isn't like the movies at all. The realization lands on me like a ton of bricks.

Mellie is still unresponsive when Vogel and Mack return. If they were fed up with me before, now they're downright livid. Even their footsteps sound angry. They look larger than life from this angle, like gods towering over us. Which, in a way, I guess they are.

"Give us the girl," shouts Mack. "Don't make me come down there."

I hesitate. I can't turn Mellie over to these madmen.

"Don't try and play the hero," adds Vogel. "This will

be easier on both of you if you hand her over. You know she needs our help. We'll be back for you later."

I could argue or make threats or force them to lower themselves into the pit to get her, but what good would it do? Mellie *does* need their help. She needs saving, even though she doesn't need The Company's kind of saving. I have to let her go.

When I hoist her up, her head rolls back, and her arms hang loose at her sides. It's like lifting a life-sized rag doll. Her eyes are still doing that fluttering thing, which is freaking me out. It's like she can see me and not see me. She's here and not here.

Just in case she can understand me, I lean down and whisper in her ear. I don't tell her that I'll save her or that everything will be fine, because I don't want to lie to her. I say the only thing I know is true. Then I pass her to Vogel and Mack and watch them carry her away.

—⚡—

Mellie

I have that floating feeling again. Trex's skin is sticky like rubber, and his arms strain under my weight. Through my dancing eyelashes, I see him one last time. Lightning Boy. The one full of sparks. He leans close to my ear. He whispers to me: "You're not broken, Mellie." It might be the nicest compliment anyone has ever given me.

Then he hands me over to the bad guys. Mack lifts me up. He still smells like puke. I chant Trex's words in my head as I sink into Mack's arms. *You're not broken. You're not broken.* With all my might I push through the tranquilizers and the pain and the dwindling consciousness. I push until it becomes movement—the slightest twitch.

"Steady, now," says Mack. "This is almost over. When you wake up, you'll be new and improved. You'll be all fixed."

But I am not broken. I am not broken.

I move my arm. I move my fingers. I might as well be lifting a car for all the effort it takes to move one limb and five measly digits. But I do it. For Trex. For me.

We arrive at the operating room—cold and silver and sterile, like a spaceship. This is where they'll change me—reprogram me, rewire me, remake me. I don't want them to *re*-anything. But they won't listen.

"I am not broken," I want to tell them.

"I am not broken," I want to tell everyone.

But I am tired. My body is tired. My brain is tired.

Every good detective knows when it's time to call a case closed.

Trex

There's nothing left to do but pace my dirt cell and think. I picture Vogel and Mack laying Mellie out on the operating table. Attaching the helmet to her head and squeezing her skull until the pressure makes her scream. Slicing into her scalp and making use of the other primitive instruments on that tray—forceps, needles, saws. It makes my blood boil, hot and sharp, like a sparkler fizzing inside my body.

But I'm helpless. Trapped. I've led Mellie to these butchers and probably gotten Mom arrested. And for what? I'll never really be normal. And now I'll never be anything but The Company's pincushion.

If I survive. The air prickles my skin, making it tingle. It might be my imagination, but I swear I can feel the electricity in the air circulating around me and pulsing. It sizzles, softly, like oil in a hot griddle. Is it the dry air doing this to me? Or is it my blood, coursing too fast through my body? Or is it just puberty, like Mom suggested? Or some combination of all these things?

Vogel said my body would eventually kill me. Maybe it's already happening. Maybe The Company's experiment has failed—again.

I can't let this happen to Mellie.

A zigzag of lightning cuts through the clouds, and I remember that night a few weeks ago, when Mellie saw sparks pass between me and the Unnamed Girl. The night that changed everything. If I had a piece of metal large enough, maybe I could change everything again. If only I could send a message. Another fireworks show.

I look around. Nothing but trees and more trees. No fences or powerlines or telephone poles. Nothing I can use to release my charge. I can almost feel the electrons bouncing off my skin. Millions of them. An infestation. But I have nowhere to send them.

Another flash of lightning blazes the sky, followed seconds later by the angry grumble of thunder. The air is still bone dry.

Dry lightning.

Mom was searching for that phrase on the computer this afternoon. After Mellie gave me access to the internet, I did a little research myself, to figure out what Mom was looking for, and now it makes sense. She was afraid the conditions in Hopewell would create dry lightning and short out my machinery. Electricity in the air, with no rain to tamp it down. A positive charge in the clouds, swerving through the sky to meet a negative one below. A rare and dangerous occurrence, with explosive results.

What if I could be the lightning *and* the rod?

A jolt like that would surely kill me.

But it just might save Mellie.

I peel off Lou's rubber gloves. I only have one chance to make this count before the police cars get too far away. I have to hold my charge, even though it hurts and the keys in my pocket would bring me blissful relief. I need a distraction. I need . . .

Action figures.

Batman.

Chocolate cake.

I close my eyes and concentrate. The sky is churning, but it's not ready yet. It won't be big or bright enough yet. I have to hold on.

Dreams.

Elephants.

Fireworks.

I stretch my hand up toward the sky, focusing all my energy into my fingertips. I'm so far away from the ions in the clouds. And so insignificant. This might not even work. And it's *definitely* going to hurt.

Ghost stories.

Hula-Hoops.

Ice cream.

Static fills my ears, so loud it brings me to my knees. A burning smell wafts from my body, and my skin makes a soft crackling sound, like a fireplace. My heart thumps as if someone is doing karate kicks against my rib cage.

Jokes.

Karaoke.

Lasagna.

The blood swirls wildly in my veins—fear and guilt and rage and shame and even love—all mixed with electricity and bubbling up inside me. I hold my arm as steady as I can.

Mom. Mellie.

A flash of blue fills the sky. It blinds me.

It's the last thing I see.

CHAPTER 50

Brick

A burst of light makes the sky glow brilliant white for an instant, like God turned on a spotlight. It stuns me. I shriek and jerk the wheel. Harrison screams from the back seat. Mrs. Chandler, beside me, squeezes her eyes shut and grips the sides of her seat. Our car careens in zigzags along the road, which luckily is deserted. In front of us, Officer Briscoe's patrol car almost swerves into a shrub.

I pull us out of the skid, clutching the wheel so hard my knuckles turn white.

"What the heck was that?" yelps Harrison.

"I think it was lightning," says Mrs. Chandler.

"But it isn't raining," says Harrison.

Both of them crane their necks to gaze up at the sky.

I stare straight ahead, but I can't see the road ahead of me. Tears blur my eyes.

"Are you okay?" asks Mrs. Chandler.

"Trex," I say. It's the only word I can manage. The only one that matters. "Trex."

CHAPTER 51

Mellie

Light floods the space behind my eyes, then dissolves into a darkness so complete I think I've died. Until Vogel utters a string of words I'm certain they don't allow in heaven. I realize I'm still here, alive, strapped to a table in a remote building in an industrial park. I've been drugged and shoved into a ravine, and now a group of evil scientists are about to perform surgery on me. I think it's safe to say this case has gotten away from me.

"What's going on?" asks Mack.

"Was that lightning?" asks the simpering doctor, Grayson.

"No," growls Vogel. "That was the boy."

Lightning Boy did *that*?

"The power is out," says Grayson. "What do we do now?"

I do a happy dance—on the inside, of course. I knew Lightning Boy would rescue me. Without electricity, these guys can't possibly operate on me. They'll have to abandon their plan and call an ambulance. Right?

An eerie red light dashes my hopes. The machines in the room begin to hum and click and beep.

"Excellent," says Vogel. "The generators are working."

"I don't know if they're strong enough," says Grayson. "These machines use a significant amount of power."

"I'm paying you five times the salary of any other surgeon in the country," snaps Vogel. "Find a way."

"Yessir," mumbles Grayson.

I'm hovering over my body, watching the scene play out like a movie. Grayson bustles around the room, adjusting dials and laying items out on trays. He's stalling. Vogel grows impatient and snaps at him to hurry. Grayson nods. He lifts a handheld machine and clicks the power on. It buzzes like a swarm of insects. The air wafting from it gently blows his hair back. Is that a buzzsaw? Is this the part where he slices into my brain to remove the Mellie parts and replace them with computer parts? He lowers it to my skull.

I try to scream, but I don't have a voice. I hold on to the one thing I do have. My new mantra. *I am not broken.*

Grayson bends over me and presses the machine into the flesh above my right temple. He moves it slowly in an arc over my ear. It doesn't hurt, but then again, I can't feel anything. Then, from my weird floating position, I realize what he's doing.

He's shaving my head. A long strip of black hair snakes to the floor. I'd cry if I had access to my tear ducts.

Next there are voices. The buzzing suddenly stops, and everyone gets upset all at once. The doctors are panicking. There's a big commotion and—

It that Mrs. Wilson?

And Harrison?

And *Mother*?

Now I'm sure I'm dead.

CHAPTER 52

Brick

Dr. Grayson drops the electric razor and backs away from Mellie's prone body. Vogel rushes at us, trying to force us out the open door. "You can't be in this room," he shouts. "It's a sterile environment. How'd you get in here?"

After the lightning flashed in the sky, I spun that car around so quickly I nearly gave us all whiplash. The surge must have knocked out the building's electricity and unlocked all the doors. A fail-safe in case of emergency. I'd say this qualifies.

"Get out of here!" Vogel shouts.

There's a low wailing behind me, and before I realize what's happening, Mrs. Chandler is rushing at Vogel, grasping him with her long, manicured nails. She tears into his neck, which is already raw. I'd recognize those burns anywhere—in the shape of Trex's fingertips—and I'm slightly comforted. At least Trex made his mark.

But where *is* he?

"Stop her!" cries Vogel, and Mack restrains the flailing Mrs. Chandler, now sobbing at the sight of her daughter unconscious and strung up to machines.

"What did you do to her?" she shrieks, casting her fiery gaze at each of the men in the room—Vogel, Grayson, Mack.

Officer Briscoe bursts into the chaos, panting. He followed me in his patrol car with his lights flashing, but he couldn't keep up. He probably rushed in here to tell me to stop bothering these nice men. But when he sees Mellie, his eyes grow wide.

"The poor girl took a spill," Vogel explains, blinking too much and clutching his neck. "We found her out back. The terrain out there is treacherous. Also . . . I've been the victim of an attack!"

I nudge Harrison, who is dazed and huddled in a corner, gaping at his bruised and bleeding classmate on the table. "Your phone," I whisper. "Start recording." It takes a moment for him to realize what I'm asking. He nods.

"This girl needs medical attention," I say. "Dr. Grayson, you are obligated by oath to help her. Her mother does not consent to any experimental procedures." I flash my eyes to Mrs. Chandler, now draped over the body of her daughter, smoothing what remains of Mellie's hair. She looks up. She understands.

"I do not consent," she says, in a loud, clear voice.

"This is . . . It's . . . it's preposterous!" stammers Vogel. "I'm trying to save this child's life, and you're making me out to be the bad guy here? This one—" He points a finger at me. "This one is a kidnapper. Did she tell you that? She's not really the boy's mother. Ask her! She stole him from a lab eight years ago. He was an orphaned patient."

"Is that true?" asks Officer Briscoe.

"Yes," I say. Everyone gasps and turns to me. Harrison trains his camera on me. "I'm ready to come clean about everything I've done, but that's hardly what matters right now. Mellie needs help. And Trex . . ."

"Where's the boy?" asks Officer Briscoe.

"I don't know," says Vogel. "We only found the girl. The boy wasn't with her."

"He's lying!" I cry. Now it's my turn to go after him, aiming for the same sensitive spot on his neck.

"Yes!" hoots Harrison, keeping his camera trained on the action.

But I stop short of wringing Vogel's skinny neck, because Mrs. Chandler squeals and waves me over.

"It's Mellie!" she cries. "She's trying to say something!"

CHAPTER 53

Mellie

I'm screaming, but they can't hear me. I'm behind Plexiglas again, pounding on it and shouting at them. I'm telling them to help Trex. I'm explaining where he is and how to find him.

But all they can see is me, barely twitching on an operating table. All they hear is my voice through a parched throat and cracked lips. "Fall . . . pills . . ."

CHAPTER 54

Brick

"What is it, Mellie?" asks Mrs. Chandler. "Did they give you pills? Is that why you fell?"

"We didn't *give her* anything," says Vogel. "We know this girl has been seeing a doctor for her . . . issues. She's delusional."

"That's not true," says Mrs. Chandler. "Mellie is the most clever kid you'll ever meet. She's trying to tell us something else." She paces the room, repeating Mellie's words. "Fall . . . pills . . ."

"Hey, check this out," says Harrison. He's crouched beside Mellie's backpack, which is slung on the floor beside her. He holds up a nondescript spiral notebook with doodles all over the cover. "Mellie is always writing in this thing at school. Maybe it's a clue or something."

"Let me see that," says Mrs. Chandler, taking the notebook. She flips through the pages, running her fingers over Mellie's sloppy handwritten notes. Tears pool in her eyes. "This is hers," she whispers. "This is . . . *her.*"

Harrison awkwardly pats Mrs. Chandler's back. She sniffles and blinks away the tears, which land on the pages and smudge the ink.

"'A good detective needs a loyal sidekick,'" she reads, with a catch in her voice. "'A good detective remains skeptical at all times. A good detective follows two things—the clues and her own intuition.'"

The rest of us nod and cast our eyes toward the floor, but Mrs. Chandler looks up and wipes her damp cheeks with the back of her hand. Her eyes glisten.

"You're right, Harrison," she says.

"Um . . . I am?"

"The notebook *is* a clue. Listen: 'A good detective *follows* two things—the clues and her own intuition.' She's not saying 'fall' . . . She's saying *follow.* Follow the pills. Mellie left us clues to find Trex!"

"You got all that from . . . the notebook?" says Officer Briscoe, raising his eyebrows.

"Look," says Harrison, darting to the doorway. He picks up a small pink object from the ground, holding it up between two fingers.

"That's one of Mellie's pills," says Mrs. Chandler.

I stare openmouthed. It's a good thing someone is cut out for this spy stuff.

"C'mon," says Harrison, hopping up and yanking my arm. "Let's go!"

Harrison and I work our way out of the room and down the hall, bent at the waist, searching for Mellie's trail of pills. I spot another one a few doors down. Harrison finds one near the back door, and my heart clenches with fear. They're leading us outside, to the dense woods behind the building.

It's all I can do to focus on the brightly colored pills—a stark contrast to the crispy brown leaves—to keep myself from thinking about why we're doing this. Is Trex tied up? Injured? Worse? I push the thoughts away and seek out the next pill, and the next.

We weave through the trees until Harrison skids to a stop. His sneaker kicks some loose stones, and they bounce down a steep incline. He's at the edge of something.

"Mrs. Wilson?" He gulps, looking down.

I steel myself and look, too. There's something down there, motionless. I can't make out what or who it is. But peeking through a carpet of leaves is the brim of a baseball cap.

CHAPTER 55

Mellie

The operating room begins to move, rocking and bouncing like someone picked up the whole building and put it in their pocket. I slide my eyes to the right, where Mother's face peers down at me, her eyes red and puffy from crying. "Darling," she says, "how are you feeling?"

I feel like someone scooped out everything in my head and replaced it with cotton balls. It doesn't hurt, exactly, but I feel more like a stuffed animal than a person. Instead of trying to explain all that, I say, "I'm okay. What happened?"

"I was hoping you could tell me." Her voice is soft, like the cotton in my head.

"I—I can't remember."

"Don't worry about that now. Just rest. You're safe."

"Where am I?"

"You're in an ambulance. You had a fall."

"Where's Trex?" I ask. The last thing I remember is going with him to find The Company. He wanted them to fix him. He thought he was broken.

"I don't know. His mother is looking for him. We found the pills you left. You were leading us to him, weren't you?"

The memories come flooding back to me all at once. The scary scientist. Trex screaming in the next room. The laced ginger ale. The ravine. Trex in pink gloves, acting like a superhero. Trex whispering to me, telling me I'm not broken.

"We have to go back!" I try to shout, but what comes out of my raw throat is more of a croak. "We have to help him." I sit up, yanking a tube out of my nostrils and tugging at the bandages taped to my wrists. An IV stand topples over. Two paramedics I didn't notice rush over and push me back onto the stretcher.

"You can't get up," one of them tells me. "It isn't safe."

The other one whispers in Mother's ear, but I hear him. "We can give her a sedative to calm her down."

Mother looks to me, and I shake my head. She takes my hand and squeezes. "No," she says. "That won't be necessary. Just let her be."

CHAPTER 56

Brick

The operating room is not how I left it. It's thick with officers now. Above the clamor of voices, the wail of sirens pierces the air. Vogel is ranting as a young sergeant leads him out of the room in handcuffs. Mack is more submissive as he's led away. Mellie is gone, the padded table now empty. Everyone is busy riffling through the room, gathering evidence. Nobody notices when I enter, my entire body smeared with dirt, my muscles sore from hoisting Trex out of the pit. He's limp in my arms, and his skin is warm. Too warm. I place him on the table.

Someone gasps. People slowly stop what they're doing and filter out of the room with their heads respectfully lowered.

"Is he . . . ?" asks Officer Briscoe. His voice falters and fades.

"I don't know," I say. "Ask *him*." I point at Dr. Grayson, who looks as though he'd rather be carted off to prison than be left alone with me. But he doesn't have a choice. It's time for him to atone for his sins. Officer Briscoe clears everyone else out of the room.

With shaking hands, Dr. Grayson straps a metal helmet onto Trex's head and connects him to various machines with a tangle of wires. He boots up a computer, and we both stare at the wobbly black-and-white image on the screen. I've been out of the game too long. I have no idea what I'm looking at.

"He's alive," says Dr. Grayson, "but his vitals are weak. Barely detectable."

"Can you save him?" I ask.

"I'm not sure."

"After all these years, that's the best you can offer?"

"I'm afraid so, ma'am. Trex's brain is designed to withstand electric input—in fact, he needs it—but the amount of energy in a lightning bolt . . . well, I don't know any technology that can handle something like that. I don't know if I can repair the damage."

"Try," I say.

I sit beside Trex and brush a stray piece of hair from his forehead. Behind me, Dr. Grayson fiddles with this and that, but I barely register what he's doing. In the past, *I* would've been the one to save Trex. But I can more easily balance a tray of sloshing drinks than read a line of code now. So I hold my son's hand and wait.

When Trex was four years old, he lay motionless on

an operating table just like this one. Like now, I waited breathlessly for him to wake up. All I cared about back then was whether the technology would work. If it did, I'd be successful. I'd be respected. I thought it would give my life meaning.

And the funny thing is, it *did* give my life meaning. Only not in the way I expected.

"It's not working, ma'am," says Grayson softly. "I— I'm losing him. There's only one option." He falls silent, but I know what he's trying to say. He stands behind me, shuffling his feet.

"Then do it," I say. "We don't have time to be timid."

"Are you sure?" he asks. "I can't imagine asking a parent to—"

"I'm a scientist," I say. "I understand the risks. Do it."

Grayson sighs. I keep my eyes on Trex as Grayson returns to his computer and types in the command. Trex's eyelashes flutter, then go still against his cheek. I've watched him sleep so many times, fretting over all the dangers he might encounter in this world. I never imagined I'd be the one to do this to him. His brain is shutting down now. He's dying.

I count the seconds that follow. Each one lasts an hour at least.

At the end of that eternity, Grayson starts clicking again. "The reboot protocol is complete," he says. "If there's no critical damage to the hardware, he should regain normal brain function within seconds."

I nod, no longer able to speak. I squeeze Trex's hand. The pulse in his wrist is so slight I can't find it, his breath so shallow that his chest doesn't rise or fall. Neither seems to be gaining strength as I wait. Just the opposite, in fact.

It's not until I notice the wet splotch on Trex's chest that I realize I'm crying in earnest, my head bent low and my shoulders heaving.

I don't know how long it's been since Dr. Grayson completed the reboot protocol. I only know it's been too long.

"He should be back by now," whispers Dr. Grayson. "I'm so sorry."

CHAPTER 57

Mellie

Father's hair is rumpled, and his face is creased. He's asleep in the vinyl chair beside my hospital bed. When I stretch, he opens his eyes and blinks at me. "You're awake," he says.

"So are you."

"I must have dozed off," he says. "These hospital chairs are so comfortable, I couldn't help myself."

Did Father just crack a joke?

"Where's Mother?" I ask.

"She went home to get you some clothes. They're going to release you in a few hours. You got banged up pretty badly, but you're going to be fine."

"What about Trex? Is he okay?"

Father pauses. I can tell he's trying to choose his words carefully. "They found him in the woods behind the building. He was hurt. Badly hurt. That's all I know right now, but the police promised to keep us updated."

"Oh." I run my fingers along the scratchy sheet draped over my legs, memorizing the weave of the cloth. Anything to keep my mind off Trex, alone in the woods. Badly hurt.

"They're going to have questions for you," says Father, "about what happened out there. But you don't have to talk to them until you're ready."

I nod.

Father reaches over and lays his hand on top of mine. "I'm sorry," he says.

"Why?" I ask. "You're not the one who pushed me into a ditch."

"I know. But I . . . I've been too hard on you. I was looking for an easy fix, instead of listening to what you were trying to tell me." He squirms in his seat, and the vinyl makes a squelchy sound. "I've always been better with numbers than people, I guess. Not that it's any excuse. The point is . . . I was wrong, Mellie. And I'm sorry."

I'm floored. I've never heard Father admit to being wrong before. Being right all the time is the one thing we have in common. After a few seconds of stunned silence, I say, "Father?"

"Yes?"

"Why don't we go to Sparks games anymore?"

The question catches him off guard. He leans back, a sad smile playing on his lips. "Because you stopped wanting to," he says. "You wanted to stay home. And eventually I stopped asking."

"Oh," I say. I fiddle with the hem of my blanket, pulling at a loose thread so I don't have to look at him. "I thought . . . I thought you were embarrassed."

"What?" He jerks forward, and I raise my eyes to meet his, which are shimmering under the hissing fluorescent lights. "I know we didn't handle things the way we should've, but we've never been ashamed of you, Mellie. We were worried about you. Never embarrassed." He releases a pained sigh.

Maybe he's not the only one who hasn't been listening. "Father?"

"Yes?"

"I think I'm ready to talk."

"Really? I can get Officer Briscoe."

"No, not to the police. To the doctor. To Dr. Colson."

Father nods and squeezes my hand. "I'll make you an appointment," he says. "I can even come with you, if you want."

"That'd be good," I say.

There's a knock on the door, and I'm grateful for it. I can only take so much family bonding. I'm less grateful when Officer Briscoe strides into the room and shuts the door behind him.

"I have news," he says.

CHAPTER 58

Trex

It's finally raining. The water splashes my face and runs down my neck, soaking my shirt. It's cooling me, and boy, do I need cooling. A single cloud hovers over me, blocking out the sky. Then the cloud sucks in a jagged breath. The cloud is . . . crying?

"Mom?"

She jerks up with a bewildered expression. Her eyes glisten with tears.

"It's okay, Mom. I'm here." I reach out and touch her arm.

She flinches. But not because I shocked her. Because I *didn't.* "How?" she asks.

"Turns out The Company has made some improvements over the years," I say. "My charge isn't gone, but it's smaller. Much smaller."

"The Company did this? They . . . fixed you?"

"Not exactly. When they hacked into me, I sort of . . . hacked them back. I downloaded all the updates for my software."

"That's why it took you so long to reboot," she says, nodding like she should've known. "You were getting an update."

"Yep."

"That's my boy!" She grins. But then her face darkens. "I mean . . . not *my* boy, but . . ."

"It's okay, Mom."

"I should've told you."

"I know. But I understand why you didn't. You were trying to protect me."

"I can't change what I've done, Trex, but I can do better. I *will* do better. If you'll let me."

"So no more secrets?"

"No more secrets," she says. She spreads her arms wide. "May I?"

I nod, and she falls on me, squeezing me in a hug and burying her head in my hair. With no rubber blanket between us, her heartbeat is like thunder. When she releases me, she flicks away her tears. "We do have some business to discuss, though. We have to decide what to do next. And I want us to make this decision together."

"I'd like that," I say.

"I know you like Hopewell, so we can stay here if you want. But that will mean dealing with The Company head-on. We can't ignore what happened here if we stay."

"I know."

"But if we leave"—she lowers her voice—"we can start over again, this time without The Company looming over us. You can enroll in a new school next semester and . . ."

"Be normal?"

"Well . . . I wouldn't go that far. But we can be inconspicuous. Nobody has to know about your brain or your charge or what The Company did to you."

I study her face—Britt the Brick, Mom. Whoever she is, she's been looking out for me all these years, when she could've walked away. What she did wasn't selfish. It was the opposite. But I still have so many questions. Questions that all the knowledge in my brain can't answer.

"I need time to decide," I say. "But first, let's talk."

CHAPTER 59

Mellie

My eyelids fly open before the sun rises, my body remembering before I do that today is a big day. I glance at the tarp and the stacked cans of paint in the corner of my bedroom. This afternoon, Mom and I are going to paint the walls Duchess Purple, finally covering the hideous yellow. But that's not why today is important.

I spring out of bed and move to the desk, flipping open my notebook. I pause for a beat, checking on each part of my body, one by one. Then I write: *Day 3, no side effects.* I twist the cap off an orange bottle and shake a small white pill onto my palm. Dr. Colson said keeping a journal is a great way to track the effects of my medicine so we can make adjustments, if necessary. And any doctor who's into journaling can't be all that bad.

It turns out Dr. Colson agrees with Trex—he doesn't

think I'm broken, either. He told me so when we had our family session a few days ago. He says I'm "introverted," which means I "derive my energy from quiet and solitude." That just means I'm content to be by myself, and Dr. C says it's perfectly normal. It's my anxiety that's the problem, and for that, he prescribed some little white pills. Considering I was able to outsmart Vogel and Mack with a bellyful of tranquilizers, I decided I'd give these a try. And they're actually helping. It appears I may have been wrong about my medication. In fact, I may have been wrong about a number of things. Unbelievable, I know.

I shut my notebook, and a flicker of movement out the window catches my eye. But when I roll my chair over for a better look, there's nobody outside. The garden is completely still. I grab my binoculars and scan the space, and that's when I spot something fluttering under the left boot of the Unnamed Girl. It looks like a slip of paper. My blood begins to tingle with the prospect of a new mystery. It's been a few days since we took down The Company, so I'm due for another case.

I grab my backpack and creep outside, careful not to wake my parents. The dawn light is just seeping into the sky, casting a dewy, dreamlike veil over the garden. I tiptoe to the statue and pluck the piece of paper out from under her heel. It's a ticket. Across the top, it says *ADMIT ONE* in big, bold letters.

"Surprise!" Trex pops out from behind a bush, followed by Barnaby, who's so excited his entire backside is lurching from side to side. "Gotcha!"

"Whatever," I say, steadying myself and pretending my heart isn't about to ricochet out of my throat. "I knew you were there."

"Liar. What will you do without me here to keep you on your toes?"

"Live a peaceful life," I grumble. "When are you heading out?"

"Now," he says. "Mom wanted to get an early start. But I had to come by and give you that." He motions to the ticket in my hand.

"What is it?"

"It's an all-access pass to every movie in the Marvel universe!" he says. "You can download them any time using the code. I couldn't leave town knowing you didn't have a basic knowledge of the MCU. It's just embarrassing."

"So now I can find out how Spider-Man got his web fingers?" I ask.

"Something like that," says Trex, shaking his head.

"Thanks," I say. "I have a gift for you, too." I reach into my backpack and pull out a stiff, spotless baseball cap emblazoned with the logo for the Hopewell Sparks. "I saw it at the game last night and thought of you," I say. "You can't start your brand-new life in that ratty old thing."

Trex removes his dirt-smeared baseball cap and studies it. "You know, this thing has been flung onto the Unnamed Girl, manhandled by evil doctors, and tossed into a ditch. Maybe it's not so lucky after all." He pulls the new cap onto his head. "A perfect fit. I'll just need Mom to make a few adjustments. Thanks."

I shrug in reply.

"I didn't know you were into baseball."

"I'm not," I admit. "I just like going to games. And the stadium sells the best kettle corn in the world. My dad and I ate so much last night that we both got sick." I grin thinking about it. It was nice, having a bellyache that was just a good, old-fashioned bellyache.

"Sounds like fun," says Trex, but I can hear the note of sadness in his voice.

"You know, if you stay in Hopewell, you can get sick on kettle corn, too."

"I know." Trex plops down on the bench. Barnaby sidles in next to him and drops his head onto Trex's knee.

"My dad talked to Office Briscoe yesterday," I add, sitting down beside him. "Apparently, the FBI received anonymous information so scandalous it will put Vogel and Mack away for a long, long time, so the Hopewell Police Department was able to drop its case against The Company. Now they don't need any testimony from us."

"Yeah, I heard that, too," says Trex.

"I'd sure like to thank whoever hacked into The Company's network and found all that incriminating evidence." I bump his knee with mine. He looks up at me with a sheepish smile. "With The Company out of the picture, you're free now. Nobody's chasing you anymore. If you ask me, Hopewell's as good a place as any to settle down."

Trex sighs. "I know. I really like it here, and I'm so sick of running. But Mom and I got to talking, and she finally told me everything. After that, I did some research of my own."

"You mean . . . *research* research?" I ask, tapping my skull to indicate his super-brain.

"Yep. And I found this."

He types something into his phone and holds it up to me. On the screen is a webpage for a place called Duncan's Auto Parts, Family-Owned Since 1988. Below the header is a photo of a group of people I assume are the Duncans, clustered together in front of a wall of hubcaps and windshield wipers.

"Uh . . . Hopewell has auto parts stores," I tell him.

"Mellie, that's my family," he says softly. "On my dad's side. The Company never contacted them after my accident, so they didn't find out what happened until it was too late. Mom never even knew they existed."

"Whoa," I say.

"Yeah. They live in my dad's hometown. Mom's hometown, too. So you see why I have to leave?"

"Of course," I say. "You have a whole family out there. I get it."

And I *do* get it. But that doesn't make it hurt any less. I don't know what to say next, and I guess Trex doesn't, either, because neither of us speak for a little while. Even Barnaby slumps to the ground. We all stare at the Unnamed Girl, and she stares back at us with that familiar, inscrutable expression.

"What do you suppose she's thinking?" Trex asks, breaking the silence at last.

"I don't know," I say softly. "She's a mystery I haven't solved yet."

"Hey," he says, not taking his eyes off the statue. "Wanna play a game?"

"Sure," I say.

"Airplanes," he says. From the corner of my eye, I see his lips break into a smile.

"Bullet trains," I say. "Do I get extra points for rhyming?"

"Nope. *Carrier pigeons!"*

"Direct messages."

"Email."

"Friends," I say, sliding my eyes to Trex.

He glances over, and for once, I think our eyes are speaking the same language. *"Good friends,"* he says.

It's like the opposite of a splash into cold water. It's like a blanket settling over me—warm and close and comforting. And just then I get another classic brilliant idea. *"Handwritten letters!"*

CHAPTER 60

Dear Mellie,

　　As promised, here is your handwritten letter. Even though it would be a billion times faster to type this out in my head and send it to your email address, a deal's a deal. But don't blame me if you can't read my handwriting!

　　My new school is pretty awesome. I joined the track team for a few days, but I quit when I discovered that running isn't nearly as much fun when you can feel pain. Instead, I started an after-school film club, and we already have 7 members. The first movie we watched was <u>Sherlock Holmes</u> (which I hear is also a book—haha!). Everyone here knows my story and has been really cool about it. Except a few kids who avoid touching me in gym, so of course I build up a big charge and give them a zap just for fun.

　　Mom found a job in a lab out here, and they're looking after my brain (in a non-creepy, non-hacking way, of course). She's back at school, too, so she can learn about all the advances in her field over the last eight years. I've never seen her so happy and relaxed. But we still play Alphabetter sometimes.

I got to meet Mom's best friend—a lady named Ronnie that she knew from her days at The Company. It was actually Ronnie who named me. She thought the word "T. rex" on my T-shirt was my name! Mom says Ronnie's a few chapters short of a novel, but I can tell she means it in the nicest way.

Most importantly, I met my biological family. My dad's parents and sister still live here, and when my real mother's family found out about me, they flew in, too. It's been crazy meeting all these relatives I didn't know I had, looking at zillions of baby pictures and home movies. I guess this is what normal kids have—big families who embarrass them with affection. But it's been sad, too, learning about the parents I never got a chance to meet. I miss them, even though I can't remember them.

But I've got Mom. She filed all the paperwork to legally adopt me, and now we're just waiting on the courts to make it official. It feels nice to stay in one place for once. I even have posters up on the wall in my bedroom, for the first time ever. And yes, they're movie posters!

My hand is starting to cramp, so I guess I should go. Write back soon and tell me all the news from Hopewell!

Your friend,
Trex

Dear Trex,

Thank you for your letter. In spite of your penmanship, it was good to hear from you! Today I found out from the Mom Squad that a new family is moving in to your old house, and they have a daughter in middle school. I bet she doesn't have a computer brain or lightning fingers, but I'll investigate her anyway.

I'm pretty famous in Hopewell these days. Nobody calls me Mouse anymore, and they're still treating me like some kind of hero. Some of the kids in drama club even shaved the left side of their head to look like mine. I didn't have the heart to tell them I didn't do it on purpose. And Harrison has been telling anyone who will listen the story about how we—all three of us!—took down an evil corporation and captured the Prowler (who everyone thinks was a goon from The Company). I haven't bothered contradicting him. I can still keep a secret.

I don't really care for fame, to be honest, but a good detective takes advantage of a good opportunity when it presents itself. So I started my own business—the Chandler Detective Agency. I've only had one case so far—helping Mr. Losh figure out who's been leaving little surprises in his front yard (spoiler—it's Walter). I know it's not murder or anything, but every good detective has to start somewhere. Also, I'm working on my memoir. The working title is <u>How to Be a Good Detective</u>. I'll send you a draft when I'm done, since you were my sidekick and all.

My parents have been really cool since The Company almost scooped out my brain. Mom and I got matching manicures, and Dad took some time off work to "reconnect," which mostly means we go to Sparks games and do puzzles together. It's been nice.

I guess that's all the news from here. In some ways, everything has changed since you showed up on Hopewell Hill, but in other ways, I'm right back where I started. Mrs. Blankenship is letting me eat lunch in the library again, and I still spend most of my time in my room, looking down at the Unnamed Girl. Let's face it, you were pretty much my only friend, and now you're gone. But I figure if I can make one friend, it stands to reason I can make another one someday. So that's something to look forward to.

I hope you'll write soon and tell me all about the continuing adventures of Lightning Boy. I'm glad he found his way home.

Love,
Mellie

AUTHOR'S NOTE

When I was in ninth grade, boarding the school bus was the worst part of my day. I was very shy, and I took great pains to go unnoticed. But during that endless trek down the center aisle of the school bus, I was on full display—or so it seemed to me. In hindsight, it's unlikely that anyone actually paid attention to me, but at the time, I felt like everyone's eyes were on me. And I hated it. I had a stomachache every morning that year.

This memory and others like it influenced my depiction of Mellie, and my own experience as an introverted child (not to mention adult) inspired me to tell this story. For most of my life, I was convinced that being shy was a character flaw that had to be corrected. From not raising my hand in class to hugging the wall at parties, it seemed that being an introvert was going to hold me back. As an avid reader, I turned to books for solace, but even there, the main character always "came out of her shell" by the last page or made a group of friends that saved her from a life of loneliness. Now that I'm holding the pen, I wanted to write a book that told introverts like me: it's okay to be who you are, full stop. In fact, your gifts—like Mellie's—may well stem from the fact that you're a little quieter and more observant than your peers.

But even as I type this, I can hear Mellie's voice in my head asking *If I'm not broken, then why do I need pills?* For most of this book, Mellie resists her diagnoses and her medication, afraid that they will change who she is. In the end, however, she discovers that taking her pills helps manage the symptoms of her anxiety without slowing her down or impacting how she defines herself. In fact, without the stomachaches to contend with, Mellie is even more astute—an even better detective. In discovering this, she makes an important distinction: being introverted isn't a problem she needs to fix, but that doesn't mean she has to live with the disruptive effects of her anxiety.

My stomachaches were never as severe as Mellie's, but back then, it was much less common to discuss mental illness of any sort. Thankfully, we've come a long way. If you're struggling with anxiety or other mental illness, help is available. You can reach out to a parent, teacher, school counselor, or other trusted grown-up, or check out resources like childmind.com. There are many ways to cope with anxiety, from simple games like Alphabetter to counseling and medication, but any treatment plan should be discussed openly, honestly, and thoughtfully with a doctor or counselor.

Most importantly, know that you are not alone. And you are not broken.

Christyne Morrell

ACKNOWLEDGMENTS

Even introverts need their people, and I'm eternally grateful for mine. Thank you to everyone who made it possible for me to go on this publishing ride a second time around:

- To agent extraordinaire Danielle Chiotti. Your expertise, guidance, and reassurance every step of the way have been invaluable. I'm so fortunate to have you in my corner.

- To my editor, Wendy Loggia. You changed my life when you plucked my first novel out of the submission pile, and I could not be more thankful. I am still awed by your ability to recognize the potential in my stories and to coax it to the surface. My favorite superpowers!

- To everyone on the Delacorte team—Alison Romig, Hannah Hill, Morgan Maple, and Jackie Hornberger. I'm honored and humbled that I get the opportunity to work with the best in the business.

• To illustrator Karl James Mountford and designer Katrina Damkoehler for this electrifying cover. Put simply, it's perfect!

• To my critique partners and beta readers— Amanda Gaspary, Amy Board, Maria Linn, Cheryl Caldwell, D. K. Brantley, G. Z. Schmidt, Kim Long, Jennifer Brown, and Amanda Proscia—not only for reading my words but for being my friends, cheerleaders, and confidants on this exhausting, exhilarating writing journey.

• To Edmund and Harper, for lifting me up and keeping me grounded at the same time. I love you so much.

ABOUT THE AUTHOR

Christyne Morrell is a children's book author and an attorney. Her first book for middle-grade readers was *Kingdom of Secrets*. When she's not writing books or negotiating contracts, she enjoys baking and watching home makeover shows. She lives in Decatur, Georgia, with her husband, their daughter, and a pampered beagle.

christynewrites.com